rumors

FROST HOLLOW
PUBLISHERS, LLC
Woodstock, Connecticut

First Edition

*Text set in Palatino
Copyright 2005 by Robert Holland
Printed on acid-free paper in Canada
ISBN 0 - 9720922-6-9*

*Robert J. Benson
Design Consultant/Illlustrations*

*Frost Hollow Publishers,LLC
411 Barlow Cemetery Road
Woodstock, CT 06281
phone: 860-974-2081
fax: 860-974-0813
email:frosthollow@mindspring.com
website: frosthollowpub.com*

rumors rum ors rumors

A Novel of Sports and Mystery by

Robert Holland

Books By
Robert Holland

The Voice of the Tree
The Purple Car
Summer on Kidd's Creek
Footballs Never Bounce True
Breakin' Stones
Eben Stroud
Harry the Hook
Mad Max Murphy
The One-Legged Man Who Came Out of a Well
The Last Champion
Charlie Dollarhide
The Black Queen
Crossing the River
Stealing
Spooks
Rumors

Check your local bookseller or order directly from Frost Hollow. Call toll free at 877-974-2081. All titles are $12 except for *Spooks*, which is $15. Shipping and handling and sales tax extra.

Also check out our web site at frosthollowpub.com. Read about the books in the series and find out what's coming next.

1 New In Town

When you're new in town and it's summer, most kids end up looking for things to do, places to go where they have a chance to meet people. And that's fine if you're pushy, which I am decidedly not. I look at it the same way I look at sports. You let the game come to you.

What that comes down to is simply putting yourself in the way of other people and because most kids are curious about somebody new, sooner or later a conversation starts.

And in as much as this is my fourth high school in four years, I've gotten pretty good at making friends in this sort of backhanded way.

But the other towns we had lived in did not have a pool hall, and I had ended up at public basketball courts and the local town beach, which was usually a pond. In Yellow Springs, which is on the coast, the town beach is a true beach. It even has a big recreation area with a full soccer field and excellent basketball courts.

but once I found out about the pool room, for nearly a month I hardly ever went to the beach. I've been playing pool for five years and I've got a great teacher. Dad. He used to win all kinds of tournaments and when I was twelve he bought a pool table, a regulation-sized Brunswick, and it has traveled with us from house to house, four houses, four towns in different parts of the country in four years.

But everybody needs competition and I decided to check out the local pool parlor.

Yellow Springs is about five towns away from the small city of Old Port where Dad works. He's now a vice president in the company and that means we're through moving unless he gets an offer with a different company. He says that won't happen because he's finally got the job he wanted, with the company he wanted to work for, but I'll believe it when we don't start packing.

The center of town is a single main street lined with old brick buildings and it's a pretty upscale, spiffy-looking sort of place. Shorty's Pool Parlor is down near the waterfront and it's connected to a bar called The Trawl Net, in an area of town that has resisted change.

The fishing boats still tie up at the docks a block away and there's a small restaurant, The Docks, where the fishermen go in the morning, and where I stop on the way to Shorty's. I'm addicted to coffee and The Docks has the best coffee in town, including the yuppie places.

It was a tough neighborhood and the clientele at Shorty's was, by any measure, rough around the edges. It's not a place I'd want to spend any time once it's dark. But it was lunch time and except for the fishermen, the place was pretty much deserted.

Still, as I turned the corner and spotted the four Harleys in the small parking lot in front of Shorty's, I felt my system jump to alert status. I always notice Harleys because that's my name, Harley Keene.

But when there's a group of them ... well, you want to watch your step because some of those biker dudes can be pretty nasty.

And though I'd been playing there for nearly three weeks, I was still the new guy, and in a local pool hall that meant I was walking on thin ice. Sooner or later, somebody was bound to step forward and challenge me. But from moving around all the time I'd learned how to deflect those challenges and how to make people laugh because when people are laughing or crying, they aren't fighting. You can take that to the bank.

It also helps that though I'm only seventeen, I'm six-foot-three and a hundred and eighty-five, and most guys don't want to get into it with me.

On the outside the building looks like a hangout for the worst, ugliest guys in town. On the inside, it's like something you see in ads for pool tables: all Brunswicks, all new, not a damaged felt in the place and there were galleries near the front four tables, which were only for tournaments. Over the door that led to the bar a sign said you had to be twenty-one to enter. But there was also a counter where you could buy food and soft drinks.

A guy about my age sat by himself at the counter with his back to the room. He wore black leathers and on the back of his jacket was a big coiled up rattlesnake. I guessed one of the bikes out front belonged to him. He also had his black hair pulled into a short pony tail and he gave you the feeling that he was looking for trouble.

I got a rack and balls and I opened my case and put my stick together. It's a heck of a stick, graphite and perfectly balanced, eighteen ounces of dynamite … in the right hands. I racked the balls, broke and began shooting, setting myself up to run the table.

Naturally, when you come into a pool hall with your own stick everybody notices. It's a sure sign that you can shoot and the only question is how well. I never play a game until I've warmed up to the point where I can run the table three times. And when I shoot pool, I focus. No choice. You have to get your stroke smoothed out until your back hand works as consistently as a machine, bringing the stick through perfectly each time.

I really get into it because you can't play the game well any other way. It's a lot like golf and in both games the ball is always still when you hit it. The only accidents on a pool table are when you miss. Every shot goes where it should and the cue ball gets left in position for not only the next shot but for the following two or three shots.

Well, that's the way you're supposed to do it, but I gotta tell you, nobody ever does it that way all the time. You can't. Not even the pros make all their shots and leave the ball perfectly set up. They just do it more often than the rest of us.

It takes a lot to break my concentration, but danger does it every time and suddenly I looked up and three guys were standing behind the guy with the snake on his jacket.

The guy wearing jeans and Nikes and a wife-beater shirt that left a lot of muscle showing, spoke first. "I hear you're supposed to be the toughest guy in this town."

The snake guy swiveled around on the counter stool and smiled. "You hear a lot of rumors," he said.

"We came to find out about you," the guy in the leathers said. The third guy, the biggest of the three, stood to the snake guy's right, his arms folded over his chest.

The snake guy shook his head. "Go home," he said, "if Jack comes in here you're gonna be in a world of hurt."

I figured Jack must be the bouncer.

"Maybe we better go outside," the big guy said.

"Won't work," the snake guy said. "Jack knows how to use doors too."

"Sounds like a wise guy," the one wearing leathers said.

They had their backs to me and I couldn't tell how old they were, but they had to be over twenty-one because they'd come from the bar. More stupid macho crap.

The thing was, they looked big and tough, but I couldn't see their faces. All I could see was the snake guy and he had these strange gray eyes and I've been around enough to know that there are some guys whose cage you don't rattle.

Guys like that aren't interested in winning a fight so much as really hurting whoever they fight. Pool players do not get into fights. It's the hands. It's all about the hands.

"We came here to settle something," the shorter guy said. "We're tired of hearing about The Snake and how tough he is and how nobody has ever beat him in a fight."

Snake shook his head. "Rumors," he said, "all rumors."

The big guy swore at him and made some nasty comment about his mother and the Snake's eyes changed. They narrowed and the smile disappeared and yet he sat on the stool, his body relaxed, while the guys in front of him had gone tense and rigid, their muscles contracting.

Here's how you play a sport. I know this because at my last two schools I've started at point guard on the basketball team and left field in baseball. You stay loose. Tighten up and you can't react fast enough.

Those guys might not have known it, but I knew they were in trouble. And then they proved it. The big one threw a punch and Snake slipped it, grabbed the guy's arm, spun him around and forced his hand almost to the base of his neck.

For the first time, I could see the big guy's face and, man, he was hurting.

"It's over," Snake said.

I think the leathers guy was inclined to agree, but the wife beater guy, who had a face like a weasel, hadn't voted yet.

"We're walking to the door," Snake said. "Slowly. If you try anything I break his arm and pull his shoulder out of joint. And to tell you the truth, I'm hoping you'll try something, because I'm looking forward to hurting somebody. Business has been kinda slow lately."

They went out into the parking lot and I dashed to the front of the room and looked out the window, watching the guys climb onto their bikes and drive off. Then the Snake zipped up his jacket, climbed onto his black Harley Fat Boy and with a great Harley roar drove away, leaving a cloud of dust hanging over the parking lot.

And that was my introduction to the guy that everyone in school called Snake. I played at the pool hall nearly every day over the rest of the summer and my reputation grew rapidly. I was the guy to beat and though I preferred straight pool, calling each shot and running rack after rack, I was also unbeatable at nine ball.

The one thing I didn't do was play for money. Dad's rule.

You only played for money in a tournament. That way you stayed out of trouble because the guys who played for money were mostly hustlers and dudes who thought they were hustlers and those guys were always on the edge of getting their fingers broken.

Shorty did not allow gambling because it always led to trouble, but some of the guys there still gambled, settling up in the parking lot outside. Most of that stuff went on at night. I played during the day. Another of Dad's rules. Trouble comes with the dark. I understood.

Even so, you meet a lot of hard cases in pool halls. I even got to know some of them, guys like Blacky Gorman, who people said was a hit man for the Mafia, and Red Dog Warren, who was supposed to have served time in prison for manslaughter after he killed a guy in a fight. And there were other guys too, guys with less desperate reputations, guys like Mike the Trapper, a big white-bearded guy who got rid of animal pests for people, and Frenchy Livernois who captained a seventy-foot stern trawler called the *Cracker Jackie*, and Wolf Wetzel, who stayed something of a mystery. These were guys who turned up during the day or I'd never have seen them. And they all had fierce reputations. Rumors. I wrote it all off as rumors. They were never anything but nice to me and they even acted as my protectors if anyone got too pushy.

I never saw Snake at Shorty's again that summer.

2 Shorty's

Maybe, if there had been some kids in the neighborhood who were my age, I'd have spent less time at Shorty's, but I don't think so. There were just too many good players there, and after I'd been playing for a couple of weeks, even some of the night guys came around in the afternoon to shoot a game or two. To get really good, you have to play against the best.

After four years of bouncing around, I'm also pretty good at being on my own hook. So's my sister Janey and she's also pretty good company, though it didn't take her long to find some kids nearby to hang with. She makes friends easily. It takes me longer.

The new house had a four-car garage and the first thing Dad did was get a glass basketball backboard and have it set up so that I had almost a full half-court blacktop area to practice on. I painted in the foul line and lanes and even put down the three-point line.

That was the hardest. I mean, did you ever try to mark out a curved line? Man, it was a puzzle. But I solved it. Heck, I like figuring things out on my own.

In the end I drove a nail into the blacktop at a point directly under the front rim and then tied a long string with a piece of chalk on it to the nail, stretched the string to the right length, and marked the big half-circle.

I won't say it was perfect, especially when I put the paint down, but it was close enough, and it gave me a first rate court to practice on, something you couldn't do much of at the Beach Club because all day long the town rec leagues played and at night the men took over the courts.

Every day I worked on my outside shot and a short jumper from the foul line. Two hours. Every day. I also pumped some iron and worked on my legs and by the end of the summer I was dropping my three-pointer at sixty two percent and I could stuff the ball pretty easily.

But some parts of my game would never improve. I would never be fast enough to keep up with the point guards who were headed for Division One colleges. On the other hand, I had a long, quick first step and I could shoot and pass and I had some serious ups. Having those options helped make up for my lack of speed.

With that and spending time at Shorty's I didn't meet a whole lot of people my age, but I figured that would work itself out once school started.

And while I was working on my pool game I heard things. It was, after all, a pool hall and people talked. And I guess the men who were there during the day liked me well enough, because after a while they began to kid me the way they ribbed the kid who worked there, Larry Farmer.

We both just laughed and let it roll off our backs. Larry went on working and I went on shooting.

One day I was working on my cross-side shots where you hit the ball off the cushion across the table and bring it back into the side pocket on your side of the table. Good players make those shots as easily as they make shots straight on to the pocket. To do that you have to practice until you don't think about what you're doing. The only thing you think about is setting up your next shot. Well, not entirely. You still have to make the first one.

I'd been at it maybe forty-five minutes, sinking each shot and always leaving the cue ball set up for the next shot, when a man I hadn't seen before, wandered in from the bar and began talking to Red Dog. He was thin and he wore a suit and tie and he looked successful. His hair had begun to thin and he had a bald spot in the back and he left his sun glasses on, but even so I got a pretty good look at him. He had a big round sort of nose and very big ears. But he didn't look sleazy. More like a businessman, I thought.

They kept their voices low and the hum of the air conditioning made it hard to hear so I only caught snatches of their conversation, a few words here and there, a complete sentence now and then. What I gathered was that the new guy had something he wanted to sell to Red Dog, but Red Dog wasn't interested.

Blacky Gorman came in and he sat down with them and I heard them laugh and then they got up and went outside. After a while Red Dog and Blacky came back in and I saw Red Dog stuff a big wad of cash into his pocket as they walked through and into the bar.

Did I know what was going on? Not a glimmer. And there's no law against carrying around a wad of cash. Still, I tucked it away.

As it turned out, a number of men like that turned up from time to time, talking either to Red Dog or Blacky. Of course I was curious but something told me to keep my mouth shut. It wasn't any of my business.

The other place I hung out was down at the docks when the fishing boats came in. All I did was watch as the men on the boats went about unloading their catch and cleaning up the boat for the next day.

Nobody seemed to mind except the captain of the *Sea Wolf*, a big barrel of a man with a full black beard. He always had a cigar butt sticking from the corner of his mouth. His eyes were black and seemed to dart like a snake's tongue and once when I was sitting on a bench along the pier he spoke to me.

"Whattya looking at?" he said.

I couldn't believe he was talking to me and I looked around.

"You! I was talking to you!"

"Me? I was just watching you unload."

"You got nothing better to do than stare at people?"

I shrugged.

"Then beat it!"

"Sure," I said and walked away. I looked back over my shoulder and he watched me until I reached the end of the dock and walked back up toward Shorty's.

After that, I always checked to see if the *Sea Wolf* was in port before I went out to watch. And I was standing there one day, watching the guys on the *Sarah Jane*, a fifty-foot side trawler, unloading flounder when one of them looked up and gestured with his head toward the entrance to the harbor where the *Sea Wolf* had just rounded the big stone jetty.

"Don't hold your breath, but here comes Black Jack Jones."

The other men laughed and shook their heads.

"What is it with that guy?" the first man asked.

"Been like that since he was a kid," one of the others said. "Always looking to pick a fight."

"How does he afford a boat like that?" one of the younger guys asked.

Several of the men chuckled but they offered no answer

to the question. The kid didn't stop. I would have. I got the message all right, but the kid wanted to push it. "I heard he was a drug runner," he said.

"I wouldn't say that out loud if I was you," somebody said, but I couldn't tell who.

For a while no one said much of anything and I watched the *Sea Wolf* come down the harbor toward the piers and the only space left open. I thought it was pretty wild that Black Jack might be a drug smuggler, but I also understood that you didn't mess around with guys like that.

I turned and walked back up toward Shorty's, slowing a little as I walked past the *Cracker Jackie*. I liked Cap'n Livernois, the guy they called Frenchy. He was younger than most of the other captains, and he always had a story to tell. I noticed the other men seemed to like him too.

Now, the boat was buttoned up tight and no one was aboard and I walked past and continued on up to Shorty's.

Cap'n Livernois was there and Wolf Wetzel and Red Dog and they were all huddled together at a table near the door to the bar, drinking coffee.

I picked up my cue stick, tucked it into its case, and walked back outside to my car and headed home.

But that was all during the summer. Later, when school started I didn't have time for Shorty's and to tell you the truth, the last few times I was there in August, I had the feeling that the men there would rather I wasn't hanging around.

Something had changed but I didn't have any idea what that might have been. And, I'll tell you, I wasn't about to go nosing around. The way it works, there are places where you belong and places where you don't and Shorty's had suddenly made my list of places where trouble lay much too close to the surface.

The last time I was there, I went with Dad to watch a local tournament. The place was crowded and smoky and there were a lot of people there I'd never seen before and some of them were pretty weird. Even Black Jack Jones was there and down toward the end of the room there was a guy built like a barrel that I'd heard about from the stories I'd overheard. Roadkill. That was his name ... really. They said he lived on meat and a lot of it came from the road-killed animals he picked up in his job working for the town crew.

I'm not sure whether I believed that or not, but seeing him for the first time, I thought it was a possibility. Twice, when I looked up, I saw him watching me, or maybe it was my imagination, but it put him high on my list of people I wanted nothing to do with ... right up there with Black Jack Jones.

For a long while after that, I played at home. Dad was a better pool player than anyone I'd seen at Shorty's. But then, I told you, he'd been a champion, traveling all over the country.

Nothing like learning from a pro.

3 Snake Stories

Keefer, the kid they called Snake, was, according to everyone I talked to at school, supposed to be as bad a dude as any bad dude in the history of mankind. Even the guys on the hockey team were afraid of him, though you never heard 'em say that because hockey guys never admit to being afraid of anyone except their coach. But you could tell he had 'em shaking in their boots because when he was around they acted like pussycats.

Keefer was about five ten and he weighed maybe a hundred and eighty and he didn't look all that strong, despite the rumors about how he took steroids and pumped iron and knew how to box and even one that said he had a black belt.

People said he was a drug dealer, that he stole cars and broke into houses and stores and held people up in back alleys and that he pulled the wings off flies and tortured small animals and even that he hated dogs.

I'm a kind of skeptical guy. I just don't believe what people tell me unless I've got some serious evidence. And anyway, I'd seen him in action, and when I asked around I found a definite shortage of witnesses, which is the usual case with most rumors, especially when the rumors run to the wild side. Granted, I hadn't seen all that much, but it was more than anyone else had seen. I knew he was fast and strong and fearless and ... well, something more too.

Some guys just have an edge to them.

To be sure, he also looked the part. He wore his leathers every day and black engineer boots and a black leather hat with a wide brim and he even wore black leather gloves with the finger ends cut away. I told you about the pony tail but he also only shaved about once a week and he had a heavy black beard.

I thought he looked cool. Kind of like a gunfighter. And he had those kind of eyes, the same kind of eyes you see on basketball players who can shoot the ball. The great Jerry West has eyes like that, and Larry Bird and George Gervin and Oscar Robertson and Michael Jordan, and hey, it's a long list. I'll bet Billy the Kid had them and John Wesley Hardin and probably Wyatt Earp.

On the other hand, he showered every day and his clothes were always clean. I know these things because Keene comes right after Keefer, and in English, history, and math everyone sat alphabetically.

The first day in class I'd introduced myself. "Hi, I'm Harley Keene and I just moved into town," I said.

He looked up at me and his eyes seemed to glow like some sort of night cat caught in the lights of the car. "The pool shark," he said.

That took me by surprise. I mean, I'd only seen him that once and he hadn't been there very long, which meant that the rumor mill had been grinding out a few tidbits about yours truly. "Yeah," I said, "kind of an anorexic Minnesota Fats."

Okay, it wasn't all that funny, but it was droll. And it had absolutely no effect on Snake. He simply turned and walked away.

That was it. Not until later, when I began to meet people, especially the guys who played on the team, did I hear all the stories, and they just didn't add up.

I kept having the feeling there was something I had missed. There was even a logic to what he did. He wore the leathers because he rode that big black, thunder-loud Harley Davidson Fat Boy. When it rained he came to school in a battered old Ford F-350 pickup with a crew cab, four-wheel drive, and a plow frame on the front, but he still wore the leathers. The truck, of course, was black.

The one message I got said this: Stay clear. And because I like my teeth and plan on keeping them for a long time, I stayed clear. But there were questions that haunted me: things that didn't make any sense, at least to me, and one day at lunch about a week before our first game of the season, when everyone at the table was feasting on the latest Keefer rumor about how he'd cleaned some guy's clock over the weekend, I let fly.

"How is it," I asked, "that he doesn't get arrested?"

Big groan. "Com'on, Harley."

"Wake up and smell the coffee, man."

"What planet are you from?"

"Get real, dude …"

I got it. "You mean nobody will rat him out because the cops won't hold him and he'll come looking for you."

Kyle Winters nodded. "You got it, man."

Well, I did, but at the same time I didn't. Call me naïve, or just dumb, but the way I saw it, the cops were supposed to take care of guys like that. Or maybe I wasn't used to living in a big town like Yellow Springs. On the other hand, how come about a dozen big tough guys didn't get him alone some night and explain how he should change his behavior?

"Anybody see it happen?" I asked.

More groans. But, of course, no one had. And the more people I asked, the more people I found who had never seen him in action.

I let it go. I stopped asking questions. I played ball and studied hard and got to know people and when the subject of Snake Keefer came up, I kept quiet.

That doesn't mean I didn't listen. In fact, I couldn't hear enough about this guy. But I repeated none of it. At first I didn't know why I did that, except that Dad always says if you're going to err, err on the side of caution. Or to put it another way, if the rumors were true then it'd be best not to ruffle his feathers.

But I could not shake the suspicion that the rumors and the guy I saw every day in class, even the guy I'd seen at Shorty's, did not quite mesh.

Well, I didn't exactly spend my life thinking about Keefer. I had too much on the line. I was busy and I had already taken aim at getting into a really good Division Three college where I'd be able to play some basketball and work toward my future, which, by the way, included law school and leveraged buy-outs. Hey, I'm a pretty aggressive guy and I'm very competitive, and taking over companies sounded like my kind of game.

Then, in an eyeblink, everything changed. One night on the way home from basketball practice I stopped to pick up the pizza for Mom, Janey, and myself. We do that when Dad's on the road, because he doesn't care much for pizza. He's a meat guy and he hates anything with tomatoes in it.

Anyway, I came out of Nicolo's Pizza Parlor, and as I walked to the car I thought I heard a sound come from the alley. A groan. I turned that way and in the dark, where the streetlights offered only indirect, dim light, I saw something move and I opened the door of the car, climbed in and turned on the headlights and there was a guy squatting next to a guy lying on his back and it looked like the guy on his back was getting robbed.

The lights stopped it and the robber whirled away and ran off toward the end of the alley. I picked up my cell phone and called 911 and then I climbed out of the car and walked into the alley ... slowly ... watching closely, listening.

I stopped next to the guy lying on the ground and then I thought I was gonna be sick. There was a great long knife sticking from the center of his chest and he wasn't moving. Just then I heard a bike start up, not just any bike, but a Harley. There's no mistaking that sound. And all I could think of was Keefer. It had to be. I listened closely as the bike roared off. Definitely a Harley.

But the thing was, everything had happened so fast that I didn't know what I'd seen. For one thing, the guy's face had been shaded by a beat-up baseball cap and he had never looked up into the lights. Worse, I couldn't say for sure how tall he was or what else he'd been wearing.

Up until that moment I had always believed that when I saw something, I knew what I'd seen, but suddenly I was swimming in a sea of doubt. A thing like that can pretty much rattle you. I mean, it's weird to think that you can't remember all the details of what you've just seen, when for as long as you can remember you had always thought that seeing was believing.

I called Mom and she and Janey came down and went into Nicolo's and ate the pizza at one of the tables and I waited outside for the cops and the ambulance. Twenty minutes. I thought that was kind of a long time, but then I'd never called the cops before so I really had no idea how long something like that could take.

They asked me a lot of questions. I had never in my life talked to a cop and I don't know what I expected, beyond what I'd seen in the movies, but it was nothing like that. These guys were perfectly polite and sure, they asked me questions, but that's their job. I mean, after all, a guy had been murdered.

I apologized a lot for not having seen more, but the guy who asked the questions, Lieutenant Colello, told me not to worry about it. He said that sometimes, later, after you get calmed down, things come back to you and he gave me his card and told me to call.

I went back inside, figuring that I was gonna be eating cold pizza, which was okay with me because I like cold pizza, but Tony had kept it warm for me. He even treated me like some kind of celebrity though all I'd done was witness a murder, or what looked like a murder, because I hadn't seen the guy get killed.

But for awhile, at school, I was pretty famous and to tell

you the truth, I didn't care for it. I guess it was the idea that somebody'd had to get dead for me to be famous and that made me feel guilty and I hate feeling guilty. I've been feeling guilty since I was born. Sometimes it's deserved, but mostly it isn't and it's like having to carry a backpack designed for a Mount Everest guide. Like, check this out. If I don't do all my homework I feel guilty and I'm so used to it, that even when I do my homework I feel guilty. Go figure, right?

So there I was, eight o'clock in the morning in advanced placement calculus, feeling guilty about not having gotten my homework done and Mr. Scully began handing back the big test we'd taken the week before.

Somehow he managed to fumble the papers just as he got to Keefer and he ended up dropping several of them and they sailed under my desk.

I reached down and as I picked them up I saw that the paper on top was Keefer's, so I handed it to him, but not before I saw the grade ... and his name. Talk about a stunner. Socrates Keefer. Guy had to have issues with a name like that. And he knew I'd seen it and his eyes cut into me like a Japanese sushi knife and then he turned away.

I'd also seen the grade and that too had left me pretty much stunned. He'd gotten a hundred: perfect. Every answer right. So what was that about? Biker dudes aren't supposed to get hundreds, they're supposed to flunk everything.

And while I sat there dumbfounded, I began to wonder whether I was smart enough to get into any college, let alone a good one. I mean, how could I not have understood that Keefer sat in front of me in three of my classes and they were all AP classes! What did that do to all those stories? Didn't it change them?

Assumptions. I'd been making assumptions about him based on nothing more than rumor and now I was faced with having to readjust my thinking … big time. You have to be smart to get into AP classes. You have to be recommended by your teachers.

And then, without any warning, I saw the image of the guy in the alley, looking up as my car lights hit him. He'd been wearing jeans and Nikes and a black ski parka … no leather, none, not even his shoes! And he was pretty heavy too, but not fat. He'd gotten to his feet too quickly to be carrying any fat, which meant he was carrying plenty of muscle and that made him all the more dangerous.

Well, there are times in your life when you make the right decision, though I was pretty sure at the time that it was the wrong decision when, after class, I stopped at Keefer's locker.

"Hey," I said, "nice job on the calc test."

He looked at me, saying nothing, just looking.

"I think that was the highest grade in the class."

"You think so?"

"Pretty sure."

"Yeah, well don't tell anyone. I wouldn't want them to get the wrong idea."

"Hey, you don't want anyone to know, that's cool."

He looked at me carefully and then nodded as if he'd made up his mind. "What'd you get?"

"Ninety-five."

"Nothing wrong with that."

"I'm gonna have to study harder, now I know I got a wizard to beat."

He laughed. It wasn't much of a laugh, I'll grant you, but it was a laugh and as far as I knew nobody had ever seen him smile.

"What's funny?"

"The wizard part. That's funny."

"I was hoping to make valedictorian," I said.

"What? A jock? That hardly ever happens."

"Whatever, but it looks like I've got some competition I hadn't counted on."

"No competition. I flunk gym."

"What?"

He grinned. "It keeps me off the honor roll."

"Yeah, that'd do it," I said, "but why?"

"Why else?"

"I'm guessing it has something to do with reputation."

"It's everything, man. Everything …"

"That why you don't use your name?"

"You're a lot quicker than the average jock," he said.

"Yeah, I noticed that," I said. "But I'm not the one named for a Greek philosopher."

"At home I'm called Soc."

I looked at him and then grinned. "You mind if I call you that?"

"Why would you want to call me anything?"

I shrugged. "Beats calling you butthead."

He laughed then, a genuine laugh, as he shook his head. But he said nothing and as he walked away I wondered just what the laugh had meant.

But that was okay with me. I like uncertainty. It gives me more room to think.

4 Reputation

I gotta tell you, having been seen talking to Snake Keefer did not enhance my reputation and it certainly raised more than a few eyebrows.

The first questions turned up at lunch.

"Okay," Tom Parks said as he opened the wrapper on his sandwich, "what's the deal here? Did you really talk to Snake?"

"Yeah," I said.

"Why would you do that?" Joe Thomas asked. "Why would you talk to him?"

I shrugged and unwrapped my roast beef grinder. I don't know about your school, but at mine we get excellent choices for lunch. "He sits in front of me in three classes."

Joe, who is one big dude at six foot six, and is our leading scorer and without question our best player, sat back in his chair and shook his head. "I'm getting a strange picture here. Aren't you taking all AP classes?"

"Just calculus, history, and English."

"Snake is in AP calculus?" Joe's eyes were so wide he looked like he'd been crossed with an owl.

"Yeah," I said. "And English and history."

Tom nearly spat out his mouthful of tuna. "He's in three AP classes?"

"So what am I not getting here?" Joe asked. "How is a loser like Keefer doing that?"

"Yeah, who's he know that gets him into those classes?" Tom asked.

"That's not how it works," I said.

Tom laughed. "Yeah, you gotta be smart, which is how I can't figure how you got into them. No other self-respecting jock is in any of 'em." Tom plays tight end on the football team and power forward in basketball. At six-four he's not as tall as Joe, but at two hundred and fifty pounds he is about as wide as a house, so while he may not have the ups that Joe has, nobody can get around him when he blocks out on rebounds and if you get him the ball inside, he can score.

"So, what's up with that?" Joe said.

"Look, we've been down this road before," I said. "You guys are gonna play Division One so you're gonna get recruited. Guys like me are going Division Three and that means I need good grades in the toughest courses." I looked around at Joe. "After all, man, I'm a guard and there's a lot of guys out there who'll eat me alive. I mean those guys are really fast and they all have great ups and all I can do is pass and shoot."

Neither of them said anything. They were embarrassed for me that I wasn't good enough to make it in Division One.

I laughed. "Hey, guys, it's okay," I said. "I know what I can do and I know that I'm not going to wind up as a professional athlete. I'm cool with that."

Joe grinned. "Sorry, man, it's just that I don't think I ever thought about anything else, you know?"

"But you should, man. You really should. All you guys have to do is work a little harder and you can get really decent grades."

"You mean study?" Tom grinned. "You're asking way too much here, dude. All you need are C's to keep the man happy."

I grinned and looked at Joe, who suddenly didn't want to look at me. "What's your father say about that, Joe?"

"What do you think? He's a doctor, you know."

"Yeah, I know. And your mother's a speech pathologist who's only taking time off to raise her family. You must be getting a lot of heat."

"I could score fifty points a game and it wouldn't be enough."

"So, get better grades," I said.

"Some people wouldn't like it," he said.

"Who? The other black guys?"

"Some of them, yeah."

"You know what's strange," I said, "is that for us dead white guys it's the girls who say who's cool and who's not, but with you guys, it's the guys who make the call."

"You gotta have friends, you know?"

"And where will those friends be when you go off to college next fall?"

"You always this hard on people?" Joe asked.

"When they're worth it."

"And you're saying I'm worth it."

I knew it was coming, the old black-white, racist crap about not letting anyone from one group include you in the other.

I headed it off. "Com'on, Joe, we play on the same team, right? You're not just a really good ball player, you're a smart player. You see the floor, you know where to be to get a pass. You work hard at your game all the time because you can see ahead and now you've started working on your outside game because you know that at six-six you have to have an outside game to play in college. You gonna take the Kaplan course for the SAT's?"

"Why would I do that?"

"What's your father say?"

"How do you know what he says?"

"He's our doctor."

"He is?"

"Yup."

"Did he put you up to this?"

"Would he do that?"

"Yeah. He's pretty desperate, I think."

"How would you feel if you were him?"

"I'd tell me to spend more time working on my left hand move."

"Whoa, whoa, whoa!" Tom said. "Can we get off this stuff? I'm getting a headache from too much thinking. I want to know more about Snake."

Joe and I looked at each other and laughed and for the first time I thought maybe I'd made a friend I'd have for a long time. Then I looked around at Tom. "There's nothing to tell, Tom. I talked to him. And you know what? He talks no differently than we do. But he has got issues, man, serious issues."

"I hear he's a crazy man in a fight," Joe said.

"But did you or anyone you know ever see him fight?" I asked.

They both shook their heads.

"See, that's the thing, isn't it? We all know all this stuff about Keefer and all of it is rumor, so in the end, it means we don't know anything about him, but we're willing to believe anything." I decided not to mention having seen him in action at Shorty's. I don't know why. I couldn't even figure out why I was defending him.

"What about those biker dudes he hangs with?" Tom asked.

"Does he? I mean, I'm asking the same question here. Have you ever seen him with those guys?"

"Com'on, Harley, wake up and smell the coffee here," Tom said. "Everybody knows because everybody knows and that's the whole thing."

"And now everybody knows that I talked to him and that's the end of Harley Keene in this school, right?"

"It doesn't help, man," Joe said. "It doesn't help at all." He shook his head slowly from side to side. "You've got to be careful about what people think of you."

"I don't care," I said.

They both looked at me as if I'd lost it.

"People are gonna think what they want, so let 'em."

"But hanging with a murderer … man, that is more than a little over the top," Tom said.

"Who says he's a murderer?"

Tom shrugged. "It's like common knowledge, man."

"Here's my take on that," I said. "When he's convicted in a court of law, I'll believe it. Until then it's all rumor."

Joe smiled, and then laughed. "Man, you talk the way you play. The guy who's open gets the ball."

"Evidence. I react to what I can see."

"You really *don't* care what other people think, do you?" Joe asked.

32

"I've been in four different schools in four years. I'm always the new guy and here's what I found out. What people tell you about other people is what they want you to believe. I make my own decisions. If I like somebody, I like him and I don't care what anybody else says." I grinned. "You meet a lot of interesting people that way."

"I don't know," Tom said, "seems like a good way to wreck your social life."

"The thing is, Tom, it doesn't. It only makes you more interesting because nobody can predict what you're gonna do next."

Joe shook his head. "You and my old man ought to get along real good."

"We do," I said, and then I looked right at him. "We both know how smart you are. Look, on the floor, you let the game come to you because if you try too hard, you tighten up and the wheels fall off. But when it comes to your studies you attack. There's no such thing as trying too hard."

"You don't give up, do you, Harley?" Joe said.

"If I did that, what would I have left?"

Joe grinned and I thought just then he looked a lot like his father.

5 Understanding

The paper said that the guy who had gotten stabbed was from out of town and was here on business and had been staying at the Waterside Inn. According to the story, the police were calling it a drug deal gone bad. That seemed to make sense, I mean those guys are whacking each other all the time, but I was having a hard time connecting a businessman to a drug deal.

On the other hand, as I thought about it, I realized that the only drug dealers I'd ever seen were in the movies, and that is not exactly a good basis for making a call.

But I did call Lt. Colello and I went down to the station because by then, nearly twenty-four hours later, my memory had begun to churn up bits and pieces of what I'd seen. For one thing, I remembered the killer when he stood up and I was pretty sure he was about five ten and wide.

I also told Lt. Colello that I didn't think he looked like a drug dealer, hoping to get him to offer more information, but he didn't react. It was as if he hadn't heard me. I let it go.

What I didn't tell him was that I was pretty sure I'd seen the guy somewhere. I mean, I guess I should have said something, but I figured unless I was sure, it was better not to say anything.

And that was pretty much the end of that. One day a man gets murdered, the next day it's in the paper and then it's gone. It was like it had never happened.

I remembered though. I remembered that big knife sticking from the guy's chest, right through his blue and gold striped tie. It was like somebody had gotten tired of his tie blowing in the wind and decided to keep it in place ... the hard way.

More than once I woke up sweating in the middle of the night, which, at first, seemed odd because I'd always thought violence didn't bother me much, but it turned out what that meant was that violence in movies and video games didn't bother me. A dead guy with a knife in his chest and blood all over the place ... that bothered me.

But only at night in my dreams and only now and then. The rest of the time I guess I was just too busy. Work. You wanna get somewhere, you work at it. There is just no other way. I suppose I always knew that, but not until I got to Yellow Springs did it really hit home. And not until school started and I started playing pickup games in the gym with the guys on the basketball team had I played in a place where the talent level was so high.

Those guys were good. They were going to schools like UConn and Duke and Arizona and Syracuse.

The last two high schools I'd been to were small and it was easy enough to be the big dog on those teams. At that level, tall guys didn't turn up much and sometimes I'd post up down low with my back to the basket and that left a guard defending me and they were never tall enough to stop my short jumper.

Here, the inside was full of trees who could run and jump and put moves on you that turned you into a pretzel when you tried to stay with 'em.

I loved it. But then we're talking basketball and there is nothing not to love. You play the game horizontally and vertically at the same time and you have to be quick and you have to see things coming way before they happen.

On the floor, even in a pickup game, you have to concentrate all the time and you have to do it while moving at full speed. By the time we started practice my game had improved a hundred percent. I'd always been able to shoot and pass, but now I was doing all that on the run, dribbling with my head up, looking for the cutter, trying to work the bounce pass into the pivot while looking the other way to throw off the defense.

I also got lucky. Yellow Springs was short on guards and their point guard had graduated the year before. Even the shooting guard wasn't all that hot because he couldn't figure out how to get himself open so he mostly just stood around. In basketball there is no standing around. You never stop. You run play after play after play and you never stop.

And when you feed the ball to the big guy in the middle and you get it to him just as he breaks into the clear, you've got a friend for life. And having a friend like Joe was way, way beyond cool.

For the first time in my life I got to know guys who had grown up way differently than I had because, while these guys came from good solid upscale families, they had to deal with a sort of underculture at school, where they were expected to act as if they had grown up in a city slum. As a result they lived two separate lives.

But on the basketball floor and when I got them alone, they were no different than me. The only difference, the only real difference between people has nothing to do with race. It's all about gender. Girls act like girls and guys act like guys. It's simple and it never changes.

Now, anyone with a grain of common sense and a course in biology ought to have known that, but somehow I hadn't. I think maybe we're not being taught the right things. But then no teacher I ever met seemed to believe that boys and girls were different. They keep trying to make them the same. Adults ... man are they screwed up or what?

I think it's the trouble with thinking you know stuff, instead of assuming you don't. It isn't even hard. You just look at what's in front of you. Girls don't act like boys. Does anybody really not know that?

Girls.

It was like a three-ring circus. I'd go out with one girl and then she'd dump me for someone else and I'd try another and that would last a while and then that would go south and, for the life of me, I could never understand why. I felt like I must have bad breath or maybe I didn't use enough deodorant, or maybe I'd suffered a pimple explosion, but no matter what I did to counter stuff like that, it didn't matter. The girls ran the show.

Along those lines, my talking to Snake didn't help at all. And we talked more all the time. No long conversations. Just a few words here and there. And then it changed.

We'd just gotten a history paper back and were standing by my locker and suddenly he asked me how I'd done.

"I did okay," I said.

"What's okay?"

"I got an A."

"B plus. That's all I can get out of Mrs. Harrison."

"She's got a reputation for giving unfair grades," I said.

"But you've got her figured out."

I shrugged. "I just give her what she wants."

He shook his head. "Easier said than done."

"There's a trick. Listen to how she talks about different

subjects and how excited she gets sometimes. Then when you do a paper, pick that subject and agree with her opinion. Use plenty of quotes and you're in."

He nodded, then looked at me with those strange cold gray eyes, his head cocked to the side. "How is it you're not afraid to talk to me?"

The question surprised me and I had no answer. So I tried a question. "Should I be?"

He smiled. "Good answer."

"Why?"

"Because it forces me to answer my own question."

I told you he's smart.

"But you won't answer it," I said.

He shook his head. "Can't do that," he said.

After that, each time we talked we got closer to some kind of understanding, or at least I thought we did. Some things are hard to know.

Then there was a second murder. Another businessman, the paper said, and once again near a pizza place. Antonio's. It happened in the parking lot out back. They found the body by the dumpster, a big knife driven through his heart.

And now Yellow Springs was a dangerous place, a place where you didn't go out alone, a place where a killer or killers hid in the dark, waiting to drive a knife into your heart. The town went from peaceful to something resembling an armed camp. Every door was locked all the time. Everybody

watched everybody else and the business at the pizza par-
lors fell off to nothing.

Slowly, week by week, the tension began to fade, mostly
because nobody else got murdered. By the time we reached
Thanksgiving break it was almost like it had never happened
and I have to say I was guilty of being one of those who
seemed to have forgotten. Maybe the way it works is that no
one wants to think about something like that.

On Friday night during Thanksgiving break we played
our first game of the year. It was homecoming night and the
game was against Welles, which had most of their team back
from the year before and they were coming into the game
expecting to clean up the floor with us. Their center was six-
nine and the guards could both shoot and the two forwards
were fast and they got a lot of rebounds.

But we were not exactly without players. Joe, at six-six
and growing, could jump over the basket and Tom took up a
lot of space inside and nobody could block out better on a
rebound. Their point guard was five-eleven and very fast,
but only maybe a half step faster than I was and I had a big
advantage in height.

What Coach told me to do was deny him the ball on defense and go right at him on offense, penetrate the defense
to draw the double-team off Joe inside.

So that's what I did. But I gotta tell you, if it hadn't been
for the conditioning I put myself through during the sum-

mer, pickup games that fall, and the amount of coaching I got from Joe, I couldn't have come close.

And their center might have been six-nine, but he was also only a junior and as often happens to guys who grow tall so quickly, the upper half and lower half of his body didn't seem to work in harmony all the time and while he could get plenty of air under his feet off the run, his standing jump was a big nothing.

When he got the ball inside, Joe stuffed him time after time. And when Joe got the ball inside he just ate the guy up either with his jump shot or with his up and under move.

I had a pretty good game. In fact that night I broke the school record for assists in a single game. All I had to do was find Joe and it was two points nearly every time. And in the second half when they went to a zone, I did what you do against a zone. First, I sank several three-pointers and when they went to a box and one, putting a guy on me man-to-man while the rest played a zone, I used my height to keep him from denying me the ball and I penetrated the zone with my dribble and dished it off.

We gave them one shot each time down. Coach Lacy is big time into playing tight defense and we played a door slammer of a defense, switching from man-to-man to zone and back and we simply shut them down.

Afterward, in the locker room, Coach told us that if we continued to play that way, if we continued to play unselfishly and worked to find the open man, we had a good shot at winning the state championship. I won't say I didn't like hearing that, but I wasn't so sure I believed it, though it was pretty clear that the rest of the guys did.

Often enough, how well you play against a team has to do with how your players match up with the players from the other team. Sooner or later I knew I'd run into a guard who was as tall as I was and had moves I couldn't stop.

Until then, I just played the game and learned and learned and worked on my shot and my foul shots. A guard has to be able to sink his foul shots because at the end of a game the ball's in his hands and the other team has to foul him to stop the clock. If you can't hit your fouls at eighty percent you're gonna wind up costing your team a game.

And once you start to win, every team that comes up against you is gonna try to bring their A game. It's like you have a target on your back. Hey, I thought it was totally cool. It's the whole point of getting to the top. I found out something else too. When it came to crunch time and we needed points, I wanted the ball. I wasn't trying to be a star, I just knew that I could get it done, that I could either score or find an open player.

By then, with each day, I seemed to move farther and farther from the murders, and especially from the body I had seen in the alley. Sometimes it seemed more like something from a movie. Life, after all, goes on and you go with it.

6 Busted

We came into school on the Monday after Thanksgiving and I think most of the kids were already starting to think about Christmas vacation, but when you play basketball, you never want school to stop because when it's out you don't play, unless it's some big deal, like homecoming.

But I gotta tell you I was floating. Hey, we'd blown the opposition away on Friday and now everybody knew we had a team.

But even with my head swelled up like a blowfish, I noticed that the atmosphere in the hallways was electric. All I had to do was listen. Here's what I heard

"Ohmygod, did you hear? They busted the Snake?"

"He's the murderer, is what I heard."

"No way!"

"Hey, it's what I heard."

"I knew one day they'd catch up with him."

"Creep like that, he could do anything."

"Just look into those eyes and tell me he's normal."

"Ohmygod, ohmygod, ohmygod!"

Well, you get the gist of it. The noise was so loud that unless you were close to someone you couldn't make out any words. It was just a buzz. So I buzzed to my locker and off to history class which was also pretty buzzy. No sooner did I sit down than Kathy Simmons who sat at the desk to my right leaned toward me.

"Didn't you hear? OhmyGod! You didn't hear?"

I shook my head. "No, what happened?"

"Snake got busted!"

"For what?"

"Nobody knows. He was just busted. It could have been for like anything! OhmyGod, even the murders! Can you imagine, sitting in class with a murderer?"

I nodded toward his desk. "He's not here," I said.

"I know, it's because he got busted!"

"When someone's been arrested, they usually say what someone was arrested for," I said. It only seemed to confuse her and just then Mrs. Harrison walked in and we quieted down. She took the roll just by looking down each aisle, noting the empty chairs, and she'd just finished when the door flew open and Sean O'Bannion came rushing into the room, put on the brakes, skidded to a stop, and then dashed to his seat.

Sean is a redhead with bright blue eyes and about a million freckles and if you don't like Sean O'Bannion then you're brain dead. Not only is he a nice guy but he is also the funniest guy I ever met.

"Do you ever look at a clock, Sean?" Mrs. Harrison asked, trying to sound stern, but nobody can be stern when they're facing Sean.

"Whoa," he said. "Clocks … what a concept."

That, of course, broke up the class, including Mrs. Harrison. For a few minutes it took my mind off Soc and what could possibly have happened, because of course the first thing that had flopped into everybody else's head was the same thing that had wormed into mine. He'd been arrested for the murders and, I gotta tell you, in just the few conversations we'd had, I knew there was absolutely, totally, no way he had killed anyone. I mean he might look like Sean Penn having a hissy fit, but that was not what lay below the surface.

I had second period free and I got permission to go out to my car for a book and while I was there I called Lt. Colello.

"Morning, Lieutenant," I said when he came on the line, "this is Harley Keene."

"Hello, Harley, what can I do for you?"

"I heard you arrested Soc Keefer."

"Who?"

"Socrates Keefer."

"Yes."

"He wasn't the guy I saw in the alley."

"Didn't you say the guy was wearing a ski mask?"

"He was. But he was way bigger than Soc, not taller, but wider."

"How do you know what we arrested him for?"

That stopped me. "I just thought, I mean …"

"Okay, let me clear this up for you. He was arrested for having no brake lights on his truck. He got a ticket. That's all. But I'll tell you, Harley, I like the fact that you were so quick to call to defend the … Snake."

"You know about that?"

"I may be an adult, but I'm not deaf, Harley, and remember this isn't so big a town as some might think. Word gets around."

"I can't believe how fast it gets around."

"But I'm glad you called. Sometimes in a situation like the one we've got here with these murders, it pays to keep your ear to the ground. People say things they don't intend to say or they hear something and repeat it. Usually there's nothing to it. But now and then we get lucky. You're in the middle of the biggest rumor mill in town, and you can do me a huge favor. What I'd like you to do is keep your ears open. Listen to what people say."

"You mean kids?" It was a fascinating notion. An adult, not just any adult, but the assistant Chief of Police wanted to know what the kids in town were talking about? Now that is a concept!

He chuckled softly. "In my line of work, it pays to listen to everybody and the thing is, sometimes it's the kids in town who have the best information."

Something bothered me. It was like he was saying two things at once and one of those things I didn't understand. So I left it in my mind as a question while I asked another. "What would I be listening for?"

"I don't know, exactly. You never do. Something that doesn't fit, maybe, or something you haven't heard before. And don't be afraid to call me. It might be nothing, but it'd be best if I had the chance to decide that."

"Okay," I said. "I can do that."

"Talk to you later, then," he said.

"Yes, sir."

Whoa. Suddenly I was a detective! I could hardly wait to get back inside the building and start tuning in. Man, I was gonna be the nosiest dude ever.

I went straight to my locker and I was thinking so hard I think my brain was smoking. I pulled out the books I'd need for the next two periods and then I heard a voice behind me.

"They hung me yet?"

I looked around at Soc and grinned.

"Took all of about five seconds."

"They're slowing down."

"You think so?"

"But you didn't."

"Yeah, I did."

"Really?"

"But I was still waiting to see what they charged you with."

"An honest man?"

"Why don't you get your brake lights fixed?" I smiled.

"That's why I was late this morning."

"You didn't ride your Harley?"

"It's supposed to snow. I'll need the truck."

"Snow?" I never pay attention to the weather. I don't care whether it's hot or cold or wet or dry. It's just what it is and I can't change it, so what can it matter?

"I make a lot of money when it snows."

I got it. He plowed driveways with the truck. Sometimes I'm dumb as a box of rocks.

"So you had to get the brake lights fixed because you had to bring the truck."

"It's part of my Dad's business. He's a landscaper. In the winter we put plows on the trucks and we plow nearly every driveway in town. We've got four trucks on the road, twenty-four hours a day if we need to."

It was the kind of stuff I would have known if I had lived here longer than five months. And yet I'd never heard anyone mention it. But why would they? Who talked about what somebody's parents did? Heck, I don't think most of the kids even knew for sure what their parents did for work.

"When is this snow supposed to start?"

"Around lunch time."

"Damn!"

"You don't like snow?" Soc asked.

"They'll cancel practice."

He grinned. "Yeah, but if they get everybody out of here early enough I can get the parking lots cleared and keep them clear so people'll have a place to park for the game tomorrow night."

"Whoa, now there's a thought."

I closed my locker and we walked down toward the cafeteria. It's a progressive school. If your grades are high you can go just about anywhere in a free period, even down to the cafeteria for a cup of coffee. It's pretty cool, being able to hang out with someone, drink some coffee, talk …

We sat at a table by the big windows, two of about ten or fifteen kids in the entire room, which seats about six hundred. It's like an airplane hanger it's so big.

"So tell me what they're saying," Soc said. He sipped his coffee. It was black and he hadn't put any sugar into it. I was impressed. Mine was almost white and had about four sugars. It was the only way I could drink it.

"You can pretty much guess, huh?"

"Let me see … the cops finally caught up with him,

right?"

I nodded.

"A guy like that, what would you expect?"

I nodded again.

"Predictable." This time he smiled.

"It doesn't bother you that people say stuff like that?"

"I'm famous. Everybody is afraid I'm gonna take their head off. Can you think of a better way to stay out of trouble?"

"You're not worried about the old gunfighter syndrome?"

"You mean being the guy you have to beat?" He shook his head. "The thing is, nobody knows. Now, if I'd been going around taking shots at all the toughest dudes in school and beating them, that would be one thing. But I'm an unknown quantity so nobody wants to take the risk. They even help spread the stories.

"Kind of rough making any friends, though."

He shrugged. "I like it this way."

"Isn't it kind of lonely?"

"Look at you? What did you say? Three schools in three years, right?"

"Four. It's four years. This is the fourth."

"What's up with that, huh?"

I couldn't figure out how he understood what sucked about having to go a new school every year but he knew all right. It meant having to prove myself all over again, though as Mom pointed out, it hadn't hurt my people skills.

"You don't mind being lonely?" I asked.

"It isn't so much what I don't mind as what I mind, and not having to deal with all the bull the girls dish out is real high on my list. I've got a goal. I'm headed somewhere and so far I haven't met many people in this school I can say the same for, especially the girls, even though they generally get the highest grades. I want to be a golf course architect."

"You play golf?"

"That's my game."

"Do we have a team?"

"I don't have time for the team. I work for my father and in the spring we're busier than a band of one-armed fiddlers. I squeeze in a round whenever I can."

"Are you taking art?"

"What, here? Forget about it. Dad's got all kinds of really sophisticated CAD programs, including two for golf course design. I figure I'll include some of my plans in my college application."

Okay, I was going a little nuts. I mean this is Snake! The baddest bad guy in the place and suddenly he is anything but, and somehow I'm the only one who knows that or ... he is the best con man in the whole country because I didn't doubt him for a second.

I looked up and here came O'Bannion under full sail and when I say full sail I mean full hair. Not only is his hair bright red but it's curly and there's a lot of it.

He cruised in, carrying a cup of coffee. "Mind if I join you?" he asked.

I looked at Soc and he grinned. "Grab a chair," he said.

Sean grinned and sat down. "I got a really good one," he said. "Becky Stovall said she heard you work for the Mafia as a hit man. She says you get contracts from some crime boss in the city and that's how come you can afford a bike and a car and a truck."

"What?" I was incredulous, stunned, as always, by such flagrant stupidity.

"Pretty good guess," Soc said.

I looked at Sean and he looked at me and then we both laughed.

"What's so funny?" Soc said. "You think something like that isn't possible? You don't think a guy my age could be a hit man?"

"Not a chance," I said. "You don't even have a full driver's license yet. Do I think the Mafia would hire a guy driving on a learner's permit? I do not."

"Ah, but you are mistaken, sir," he said. "In fact, because of the business, I have a commercial license. And as to the matter of hit men, wouldn't it be logical to hire someone most people would never suspect?"

"I think I have to leave now," Sean said. "My mother's been real clear on this. I run into any high crime guys, Mafia family members, made guys, anybody in shoes with pointy toes, shiny suits, and slicked back hair, I'm supposed to run."

"Relax," I said to Sean and then looked across at Soc. "Maybe it could happen, but you're probably the most high profile guy in the whole town. You'd be the last guy they'd hire."

Sean grinned. "On the other hand, it makes a great rumor."

Soc shook his head. "By this afternoon half the school is gonna think I'm working for the mob."

"You got that right," I said. "Doesn't that bother you?"

"Reputation is everything," Soc said.

Just then the bell rang and we finished our coffee and dropped the cups in the trash basket on the way out of the cafeteria.

"Tell me," Sean said, "how's the pay? Because I been looking for something part time to cover my car insurance and, hey, jobs are hard to find now that my folks won't let me deliver pizza."

"I'll have Louie give you a call, something comes up."

He walked away and Sean and I walked off toward the gym for another round of the most idiotic class in school … co-ed gym. I mean what sense does it make to require a guy who plays two sports to take gym? And it makes no sense at all to have girls playing in the same game as guys.

Not that there aren't girls who can play sports. I mean, don't get me wrong here. There are girls who are great athletes. But when you put them into a game with guys one of two things happens: either they get hammered, or the guys back way off and just goof on everybody. What it amounts to is another dumb adult attempt to make everyone equal when everybody knows they're not.

Most adults seem to think that boys have a corner on the dumb market, but the truth is, we see things like that for what they are: stupid! And how are you supposed to have respect for adults when you know that most of them are two sandwiches shy of a picnic?

"You don't think it's possible, do you?" Sean said.

"Yeah, right."

"But it'd be a smart move," he said. "Who'd think a kid was a hit man?"

"Becky Stovall," I said.

He grinned. "But not the cops."

"No," I said. "Not the cops." I grinned. "And especially not anyone who knows Soc."

"You gotta like the rumor, though," Sean said.

"Stuff like that always backfires."

He grinned. "You're right. Just look at me. I'm always in hot water of some kind. I'm a perpetual backfire." He pointed to his bright red hair. "Even got the hair for the job."

7   Apple Pie And ...

The snow held off, starting at ten-fif-teen or so the next morning and it went from nothing to a blizzard in an eye blink. All you heard was talk about how there wouldn't be any school tomorrow and how we were supposed to get at least two feet of snow and hey, missing a practice was one thing but now, if they cancelled school the game would be postponed.

So, by the time I got to math and plunked myself down into my seat I was feeling pretty low. Stupid, I know, but once a team gets into a rhythm, and we were totally in sync, one missed game can throw your timing off and it might take a full half to get it back.

Then they announced that school would be closing at noon and I kind of slumped into my seat and waited to leave, while all around me kids acted like school had been closed for the year. And this was an AP class, where you'd think people liked school. Naw. Nobody likes school. They go and they either do well or they don't, but nobody likes having to study and having people telling them what to do.

I know, I know, I've heard it since I can remember. All the work pays off later. High school is brain training for college and college is brain training for getting a good job. Heck, it might even be true, and while I'm not real clear on why I should believe what adults tell me, I gotta admit, much as it galls me, that sometimes they get it right. They've even got evidence. They're successful. And the ones who aren't are the ones who didn't work when they should have, or at least that's what adults say.

Stuff like that is kind of like the evidence judges won't allow in a trial when they label it hearsay. On the other hand, I learned to shoot pool by working at it. I learned to play basketball and baseball by working at it. Is this getting boring? Probably. It sounds kind of like a lecture. I hate lectures. They make me squirm, so I'll get off this subject, but I'll leave you with this. I get high grades by working. Enough said.

I dragged myself along to my locker and gathered up all the stuff I'd need, feeling pretty crummy because I kind of live for basketball. Just then Soc slammed his locker shut, looked over at me, and shook his head.

"It's only snow," he said.

"I know. I just hate having it get in the way."

He laughed. "What I do is get it out of the way. And I get paid for it."

"For every down there's an up, right?"

"Seems like it." He slung his back pack over his shoulder and I joined him and we started for the door to the parking lot.

"Hey," he said, "how about I come pick you up when I start plowing and you can ride along with me for awhile." He dug into the pocket of his leather jacket, pulled out a small black book, and opened it. Your place is on my list. I'll call and tell you when I'm gonna get there … if you're interested."

I was. In fact, it sounded like it might even be fun. "Yeah," I said. "That'd be cool."

Mom's reaction was predictable. "What? You want to go snow plowing with Snake Keefer? Do you know who he is? Did you know he got arrested last night? No. Absolutely not!"

I didn't get mad. What would have been the point, besides she was only trying to protect her son and as much as I hated that, I was seventeen and hey, you get older, some things you start to understand. And besides, Mom needed a lot of room. Not only did she have three kids to take care of, but the moving had not been easy. The packing alone had taken four months out of her life and the unpacking had taken another four.

I poured myself a big mug of milk and cut a piece of the fresh apple pie Mom had baked just for us when we got home from school (now, how can you get mad at someone who does that?).

"His real name is Socrates," I said between bites. Mom makes the world's best apple pie. "And he's in three of my AP classes." I didn't mention the scene in Shorty's, I mean, there are some things that mothers don't understand and fighting is very high on the list.

Actually, avoiding a fight is pretty high on my list too. The last time I got into a fight I was nine and that's when I discovered that I'm a lousy fighter. I can't even remember what that fight was about. All I remember is the bloody nose and the anger, and then thinking how much I wanted to knock the kid's teeth down his throat.

Instead, I'd spent two hours shooting hoops and working on my ball handling skills. That was when I really began to like basketball.

"Snake Keefer is in your AP classes?" Mom asked.

"He's really smart. He gets hundreds on the math tests."

"Really?"

"Yup."

"Then how do you explain all the stories?"

I shrugged. I mean, I didn't know the answer to that and to tell you the truth, there was a lot I didn't know about Soc.

So, I shrugged. Didn't work.

"What are you not telling me here?" Mom said.

"Just that he's not what the rumors say he is. It's like there are two Soc Keefers. One is the guy in the rumors and the other is this great student."

"And he gets A's?" Mom, like Dad, is smart. She went to Trinity and he went to Bowdoin and they met at a football game. She has her masters in theater, too, but I always forget where that's from. Instead of working, she stayed home to raise her kids and that's one thing I am never going to forget. I probably would have, but Dad has made a point over the years of making sure that we understood why our lives were better than a lot of the kids we grew up with.

"Are you sure we're talking about the same guy?" she asked.

I grinned. "Nobody believes it," I said. I went for another round of pie and milk.

"Well, after all the stories I've heard, who would?"

Mom has a knack for getting to know people very quickly. It comes from all the moving around.

"I'm not saying he's not different, because he is, and that's for sure. But most of it's just an act."

"But not all of it."

"He can handle himself," I said. Dangerous ground. I knew it, but I seemed unable to resist.

"And how would you know that?"

Well, there it was. Put up or shut up. "This summer when I was shooting pool he was there. I didn't know who he was, but three guys came into the place looking for him and they wanted a fight. Before they could blink he had one of them in a really nasty hammerlock and he pushed the guy outside and it took the wind out of the others."

"Wonderful. My son has taken up with a very intelligent thug. Is there something wrong with this picture?"

"Mom, all he did was defend himself and he was really cool about it. No fuss, no big fight. He just handled it."

She poured herself a cup of coffee and sat at the table. "I looked up the list of who was on high honors last year and I don't remember seeing his name."

"He flunks gym."

"How can you flunk gym?"

"On purpose. That way his name never turns up on the list and he can go on convincing people he's some kind of bad-ass dude." (You're probably wondering how I could use that word around home, but we're a pretty liberal family with mild swear words ... as long as we don't get carried away. And besides, you hear it all the time.)

"Why would he do that?"

"So no one will pick on him. He says the bullies won't have anything to do with him and the teachers don't expect anything from him so they stay off his case. He told me that in his academic subjects he's never gotten less than an A."

"He sounds like a tremendous actor."

"He is. He's got the whole place buffaloed."

"How come you weren't taken in?"

I went for a second piece of pie and more milk. "By accident I saw his grade on a math test. He got a hundred on it. I got a ninety-five. And when we got to talking, we found out we get along."

"What about the arrest?"

"The brake lights were out on his truck. Actually, it's his father's truck. He owns Green Things Landscaping. Soc plows snow for him in the winter and runs all sorts of machines the rest of the year. And, get this. In his spare time he plays golf and designs golf courses. He wants to be a golf course architect."

She smiled and laughed. "Now that's different. He almost sounds like our kind of guy."

"Wait till you meet him."

Of course, I could have been lying, I mean, sometimes kids do that, but I wasn't and she knew I wasn't and the reason she knew that was because I almost never lie to my parents. I won't say I'm perfect about that, but I'm pretty close. Why? Because Dad and Mom don't lie. They have always told us the truth about things and they expect us to tell them the truth. I won't say that's always been easy, and I can't even say for sure that it always got me where I wanted to go, but there's this to be said. I never have to think about what I'm going to say.

There's even a bigger benefit. Because they know I'm not lying, they've always been willing to listen to my explanations, to talk things over, and come to a conclusion that fits the situation.

That's worked fine with both me and Ward, but Janey is another case. She's a little like a volcano. And to see her go off, all you have to do is say no. Woosh! Big time argument. Then I go try to get her quieted down. But hey, she's a girl, and they get pretty emotional about almost anything. She turned thirteen this summer and that didn't help much either, except that more and more now when I sit down to talk with her, she listens. She even leaves the door to her room open and joins the conversation at dinner.

This fall, Mom started her in private acting classes at the state university and that made a huge change. Hey, we all find ourselves in different ways. For Ward it was a soccer ball, and I gotta tell you he is one awesome sweeper, probably All-American. At Bowdoin this year he started as a freshman and they have a great team. For me it's a basketball. For Janey it looks like it's the stage. But it could also be basketball because she is very tall for thirteen and she is a really good athlete. It kind of runs in the family. And we all support each other. It's the way my family works.

Do we always get along? Hey, there's no Garden of Eden. Well, there isn't. We have some major league ups and downs. Then we adjust. Like the bumper sticker says: "We're all dysfunctional … get over it!"

"Have you heard a weather report?" I asked.

"Twelve to sixteen inches."

"Is Dad coming home?"

"He's on his way. Thank God he bought the Landcruiser."

Just then my cell phone rang and I answered it. "Yeah?"

"I'm on my way over," Soc said. "Looks like an all-nighter. You ready for that?"

"Sure."

"Pack yourself some food and a thermos of coffee and we'll plow some driveways."

"How long?"

"Twenty minutes."

"I'll be looking for you." As I switched off the phone I realized that Mom hadn't said I could go. I looked over at her. "Is it okay?"

"Sure, why not?"

"It also means we'll get our driveway plowed early."

"We already have somebody for that."

"I know. Dad hired Green Things. We're on Soc's list. He'll plow us out when he gets here and then we'll be up all night."

"All night?"

"It's okay, Mom. No school tomorrow and that means no game."

She could see I was excited about spending a night out plowing through the storm and she grinned. "I guess it's doable," she said and then got up. "You'll need some food and a big thermos of coffee."

Hey, are Moms great or what?

Then she said: "This is pretty dangerous stuff, you know."

I nodded. "Soc's been doing this since he was a boy. And the truck has all kinds of emergency equipment, including radios and a GPS tracking system so his mother can locate any truck at any time."

"How about blankets?"

She finished with the coffee and walked to the fridge.

I had no idea, but I didn't lie. "I don't know but I'm pretty sure he's got something."

I ended up adding a sleeping bag to the stuff Mom required. No argument. In the winter with the temperature around twenty, you go prepared. End of story.

8 Talking To A Stranger

I climbed into Soc's truck. I should say I climbed *up* into the truck because it was a long way off the ground. The interior surprised me considerably. I had expected worn out seats and a ratty old floor with some holes through it and instead I dropped my tail down onto a heated leather captain's chair complete with armrests. The floor was carpeted and there was a CD player and even the back seats were leather.

Outside, it was a work truck with a plow and a sanding machine in the eight-foot bed. Inside, it was like somebody's living room. You could hardly hear the big diesel engine up front.

"Whoa, nice truck," I said.

Soc grinned. "Yeah, well I spend a lot of hours in this old beauty and I decided to fix it up some. It's all about the comforts, man."

He had plowed his way up the long drive and now he

swung the plow and pushed the snow off to the side, leaving it at the end of the turnaround. It took him only minutes to clear the rest of the driveway and he never made a false move.

"Man, that was fast," I said.

He backed down to the street, cleaned up the entrance to the drive with two swipes, and went on to the next house.

"It takes a while to get the hang of it," he said, "and on a night like this you need a lot of endurance. I'll have to plow at least twice on all the drives I do over the next four hours."

There are ten houses on our road and he plowed them all in what seemed an incredibly short time.

Geographically, Yellow Springs is a pretty big town and once you get outside the center, the houses are spread out, and some of them have driveways so long they're more like roads.

We talked and I watched and I was having a great time and I was also learning a great deal about how you plowed snow the right way, meaning you used as little fuel as possible and put as little pressure on the equipment as possible. Soc explained it all in great detail as we went from driveway to driveway.

"I've plowed all of these places for the past two winters," he said, "and that helps a lot. I know where to pile the snow so when the next storm hits I can pile more snow."

"How come you plow the town road ahead of each driveway?" I asked.

"Special service. No sooner do I get a driveway cleared then the town or the state plow comes along and lays a berm across it. So last winter I began making an indentation about twenty feet from the driveway so that the snow the plow is carrying slides off into the space I left and that reduces the size of the berm at the driveway.

"But I only do that where the people don't have an SUV. Those guys love busting through the plow berm. It's about the only time they get to use four-wheel drive."

I had to laugh.

"What's so funny?"

"You got my old man absolutely pegged. He's been waiting for a snowstorm so he could test out his Landcruiser."

"That's why I didn't make a cut ahead of your driveway."

"Do you always know stuff like that?"

He tapped his head. "I make notes. I was cutting the lawn next door last summer when he came home with the Landcruiser."

"Well, that's pretty cool," I said.

So on we went and it kept on snowing. And now the wind had picked up and sometimes it was almost impossible to see with the big plow lights reflecting back off the snow. I had no idea where we were. I might as well have been on a ship at sea.

But Soc just kept on plowing snow. And when he hit a road that the town plow hadn't reached, he dropped his plow and cleared the road. "The union guys don't like it when we do that," he said. "They think it takes work away from them, but if they'd get their job done, we wouldn't have to. I'm not about to have one of our customers get stuck on a road that should have been plowed by now. Those guys take their time because it's all overtime money when a storm hits the way this one did. They didn't even start to plow till four. Dad tried to get the town to hire independent contractors but the union threatened to strike.

"Then the school board hired us to do the schools because the town guys never got there in time. They're too busy plowing the roads where all the politicians live."

"I never heard any of this," I said.

"We're kind of in the middle of it."

"Didn't the union object to your plowing out the schools?"

"Sure. And the Board of Ed said the town could do it if they'd guarantee to do the schools first. But, of course, they couldn't agree to that so the Board hired us and we never miss. Some days we have to plow town roads the whole way just to get to the schools."

I laughed. "Which means the busses can run because you guys are on the job. Not a popular idea with most kids, I think."

"Probably not."

Then for awhile we just cruised along, from place to place and little by little I began to think that it didn't look so hard.

"What do you think about the murders?" Soc asked.

"I saw the first guy, you know."

"I heard that."

"It was awful, man. There was a lot of blood and he had a big knife sticking straight out of his chest. I saw the guy who killed him too, but I didn't get a good look at him. He ran off and then I heard a motorcycle start up and take off in a hurry."

"Really! What kind of a bike was it?"

"It sounded like a Harley."

"You know much about bikes?"

"Nothing."

"Damn, I wish I'd been there. I could've told you if it was a Harley. Probably could have told you which model."

"You can tell that?"

"Most of the time. I mean, it's not perfect, but I could have narrowed it to a couple of models."

"Who do you think the guy is?"

"No idea." He laughed. "But everybody at school thinks I did 'em, right?" He laughed again. "I'm a better actor than I thought."

I waited.

"You don't believe me, do you?"

"I believe you."

"But I'll bet when you heard that bike start up, you thought I'd done it."

"Hey, I'm not gonna lie. But I didn't know you then either. And I'm new here. It takes a while to sort things out. You got people saying all kinds of stuff and there's no way to know if any of it's true." I laughed. "But then I actually know something about you that nobody else seems to know. This summer I saw you take those guys at Shorty's to school."

"I wondered if you remembered that."

"Yeah."

"Guess I'm busted, then."

"What's that mean?"

"That maybe I really am some kind of bad-ass dude."

"Looked like it to me."

"I got two older brothers in the Marines and my Dad was a Marine. They taught the little guy a few tricks, that's all." He laughed. "Well, maybe a lot of tricks. Good stuff to know."

"My answer to defending myself is not to get into a position where I have to defend myself."

"Good policy."

"But the rest of it is all rumor."

He chuckled. "And then you saw my grade on the math test and that blew my cover."

"Pretty much, yeah."

"You really are a lot smarter than the average jock."

"That's because I'm only an average jock."

"That's not what I hear."

"It's true, though. Division Three. No higher. It's all about who you're playing against. In this league it's mostly white guys so I match up and I have a height advantage. But when I'm up against a black guy who is fast and has serious ups, it's gonna be a long night. Joe knows. It's why I spend most of my time learning to pass better."

"You always so objective about yourself?"

I shrugged. "Sure, I guess so. Never thought about it much. You know how that works."

"Yeah," Soc said, "yeah, I do." He turned into yet another driveway, a long one, and with the snow you couldn't even see the house lights. It seemed to go on and on, though it was hard to judge the distance because of the snow and our speed. But there were tracks through the snow that looked recent.

"Looks like somebody made it through," I said.

"Probably the caretaker."

Still the road wound on ahead, twisting through the closely set pines.

"Man," I said, "does this thing end?"

"A couple of hundred yards more. Old man Henry lives here. Probably the richest man in town. He's away in the winter, but the caretaker and his family live here year round.

Barney Varney. Bad name, nice guy."

We both laughed.

"You know what the murders look like to me is some kind of turf wars," Soc said.

"I thought they were men here on business."

"Yeah, well, things are often not what they seem."

At the end, the drive fanned out and Soc cleared the circular part in front of the house and then cleared the parking area and finally the drive that led to Barney Varney's house, set back in a clearing and screened from the main house by the trees.

Varney's truck was parked in the garage and the lights in the house were on and Soc made short work of the snow, and, as always, swept the berm away from the garage entrance.

Finally, on the way out, he widened the driveway on the right hand side out to the main road. We turned right and hadn't gone a half mile before, through a sudden gap in the snow, I saw someone run out into the road and start waving his arms at us. "Whoa, what's that?"

"Got me. Under the seat there's a short iron bar. Get it out just in case."

Everybody thinks they're brave. Everybody thinks they'll be cool as ice when the crunch comes, and I'm no different … except that I was shaking and I thought I'd piss my pants any second as Soc slowed and wound down his window.

There wasn't a house anywhere.

"What's the problem?"

"My car ran off the road," the guy said, "and my cell phone's dead. I don't even know where I am!" He was wearing a top coat, wrapped tightly to his throat with the collar pulled up and he had on a baseball cap with no logo on the front and it looked pretty battered.

"Backer's Hill Road," Soc said.

We could see the roof of the car, well below the road, and the tracks where it had gone down the embankment.

"Is anybody hurt?"

"No. I'm alone."

"I'll call for a wrecker. I'd twitch you out but I can't stop for that just now. Too much snow. I'll tell them exactly where you are."

"You can't go off and leave me here!"

Soc looked at his fuel gauge and nodded. "Then I'll give you a lift. Even if they pulled you out, the snow's too deep for you to go anywhere and once the car's back up on the road there's a chance the town plow won't see it and that'd pretty much be the end of your car."

He picked his cell phone from the holder on the dash and checked in with his mother so she'd know where he was then put the phone back into the holder. "You live in town?"

"No. I was headed for The Waterside Inn."

"Climb in. I might as well refuel now as later."

The man pulled the back door open, climbed in, and slid across the set until he was directly behind me. I sat half-turned in my seat so I could keep an eye on him. Hey, what is it your parents always say? Never talk to strangers? Well, there we were with one in the back seat and there was, after all, a murderer running amok. I wrapped my fingers tightly around the iron bar.

Maybe if Soc's truck had been the extended cab type I could have seen the guy in the lights from the dash. But it was a crew cab and he was sitting well back into the seat. All I could see for sure was the baseball cap and his nose and chin. It looked like he hadn't shaved but again, a thing like that is hard to be sure of. Some men have heavy beards and need to shave at least twice a day and here it was, the middle of the night, so if he'd shaved that morning, he could easily have been showing a lot of whiskers.

Soc dropped the plow and cut a track over the hill down to Plum Road, which the town had just cleared.

"Guess I shouldn't have tried to make it through," the man said. "It seemed okay when I started and then I got out here and the snow was so thick I made a wrong turn."

"Easy to do," Soc said.

"I'm just glad you came along when you did. I might have frozen to death."

"All you had to do was walk to the end of the road. There're plenty of houses."

"I didn't want to leave the car."

"Well, you can get it in the morning. Call Tasker's. If they're not too busy they'll get it out tonight and tow it into the village for you. Tell him Soc Keefer said to call. Be best if they got it out before the snow gets too high on the side of the road."

"You guys'll be plowing all night won't you?"

"Most likely," Soc said.

"Heck of a storm …"

"You come this way often?" Soc asked.

"I'm here at least once a month on business, sometimes twice."

"What kind of car you driving?" Soc asked.

"A Mercedes." He grunted. "But after this I'm thinking I need something with a little better traction."

All the time this was going on something was beginning to bother me. It was like an itch I couldn't scratch, an idea that slithered away like an eel each time I got close. I squirmed in my seat. And now I had an urge to keep him talking.

"Where did you come from?" I asked.

"Yesterday I was in Bing, the day before that in Upland City."

"No, I meant where's your company?"

"Upstate New York. Syracuse. We're a subcontractor for Argus."

What he said sounded perfectly logical and yet … there

was that unscratchable itch again. Call it instinct, call it intuition, call it anything you want, but I knew as sure as orange juice comes from oranges that something was wildly askew.

And then, only faintly, above the roar of the big diesel engine I heard the unmistakable rumble of a cell phone set on quiet mode. It wasn't mine. It wasn't Soc's. But this guy had told us his phone was dead.

After that the conversation died off and nobody said anything until we stopped at The Waterside. He climbed out, thanked us for the help and we headed over to Soc's to fill up before heading back out into the storm.

When we were back on the road, I turned in the seat. "Didn't that guy say his cell phone was dead?"

"That's what he said."

"Well, it wasn't. I heard it rumble in his pocket."

"Maybe it had a small charge left in the battery."

"Maybe."

"But you don't think so."

"Nope." I pulled out my cell and called Lt. Colello and told him about the car off the road and the story about the cell phone and he said he'd check it out.

"You've got an in with Colello?" Soc smiled.

"Because I was a witness."

"He's a good guy, you know."

"You know him?"

"He's my godfather."

"No way ... your godfather's a cop?"

"He's pretty cool."

"Even so, it's kind of weird."

"What you see is what you get. That's Nick. And he's an absolute tiger when it comes to the law." He laughed. "Even gave his godson a ticket."

"Whoa, that's harsh."

"Naw. Just fair. No favorites with Nick. You break the law, you pay the price. And another thing. You'll never get hassled by a cop in Yellow Springs. They behave just like the State Troopers. Always polite."

"He asked me to keep my ear to the ground at school."

"Really? That's a first. You must've made a good impression."

"I just told him what I saw."

"And by inference, what you didn't see."

"I didn't want to send him off on some kind of wild goose chase."

"How do you do that?"

"What?"

"Not exaggerate."

"No imagination."

"Not likely."

"Why do you say that?"

"Because I've seen you on the basketball court."

Well, I had no answer for that and I let it go.

All night we plowed and talked and laughed and by first light I discovered that I'd made as good a friend as I'd ever had. We just hit it off. We laughed at the same things. We liked and disliked the same teachers and Soc even convinced me to try golf in the spring.

The only surprise, and it was something more than a surprise, came when we went back over Backer's Hill to re-plow two driveways on Plum Road.

By then the storm had pretty much blown itself out and as we came over the top of the hill and started down, there was the Mercedes still off the road.

"I can't believe John Tasker hasn't gotten here," Soc said, as he slowed the truck to a stop, peering through the windshield. "I don't see any tracks so I don't think Nick got here either. Let's take a look."

We climbed out of the truck and over the berm and down through the knee-deep snow to the car and stood there staring through the window at the body of a man in the passenger seat with a big weird knife sticking straight out of his chest. I'd seen a knife just like it before and I knew only too well where.

"Are you thinking what I'm thinking?" Soc asked.

"Yeah, I'm thinking that we had the murderer right there in the truck and we're still alive and I can't figure out why."

Soc took out his cell phone and called Nick. After that we hiked back up to the road, cleared the berm away so the wrecker could drag the car free, and waited in the truck.

"Man that is ugly," Soc said.

"I can't believe I've seen two out of the three victims."

"Pretty weird," Soc said.

"I think I'd rather not see any more," I said.

"Me either," Soc said.

"Why didn't he kill us?"

"I think he was either scared he'd freeze to death, or he ran off the road and just wanted to get away."

"And he couldn't stay with the car, could he?"

"Not with the body there."

Soc shook his head. "Did you get a good look at him?"

"His face was hidden by his hat."

"What a couple of dupes," Soc said. "And I thought I was pretty smart, too."

"Smart has nothing to do with it," I said. "It's a matter of experience. Maybe if we'd met more murderers, we'd have spotted him for what he was."

Soc laughed. "So, does this mean we need to visit the state prison more often?"

"Probably not," I said. And then suddenly the chills danced up my spine. "You know, we have a problem here," I said. "We've seen him and he doesn't know what we saw."

"Which means he might think we could identify him."

"Not good," I said.

"No. Not good at all," Soc said. "Here's the worst part.

There was something familiar about him."

"Yeah," I said, "there was."

"Which means he's probably local."

"And he knows us."

"Yeah."

"This just gets better by the second."

Soc grinned. "Nothing like a nice quiet night of plowing snow."

9 Bad Break

The only thing I have to say about the conversations we had with the police, was that admitting I'd seen two of the victims just after they'd been killed made me pretty nervous. And I'm only going to mention the dreams I had, which now turned up whenever I closed my eyes. Who wants to hear gruesome stuff like that?

Basketball. The next game was on Friday, after the snow had wiped out the game on Tuesday. It's a stupid rule. If they close school for the day then they cancel all the sports. Of course this time it made sense. Soc and I had been plowing all night and when we quit it was still snowing, so nobody could have gotten to the game.

I didn't wake up till supper.

The next few days at school were really weird. The story was out that we had found the murdered guy and now it was clear that Soc was not the murderer, which meant that people had to look elsewhere, only there was nowhere to look. It's one thing to be afraid of a murderer when you know who the murderer is, but it's altogether different when you don't know because then it could be anybody.

There's no logic or even common sense here. I mean, did anyone really think the killer was hanging around the school? Did anybody even think? I remembered a scene from a movie where a fox got into a chicken yard. That's what it was like at school. The gobbling and cackling never stopped. Even the teachers fell prey to it. The only thing missing was all the feathers and dust in the air.

And whenever Soc and I came near, all the gabbing stopped and they watched us as if we had stepped fresh out of an old boneyard. Part of that may have been that I was hanging out with Soc, which wasn't doing much for my social standing in the community, but by then I didn't have all that much to lose. I was the starting point guard and the guys on the team knew what I could do. They also knew that I got 'em the ball, and when you're looking to go Division One you need numbers and I was the guy that could get them the numbers they needed. A thing like that can make you popular ... fast.

We tried to ignore the rest of the kids, all whispering and round-eyed as they stared, but I gotta tell you, it wasn't easy. It's like forgetting to put your pants on and going out in public, not that I've ever done that, for gosh sakes, but you get the idea. Makes me shiver just to think about it.

Friday night we played Blessington High, not one of the hot teams in the league, exactly, but they did have a point guard who played wicked defense and made my life miserable. He was fast and he could jump and he had really quick hands, so I had to use my body to protect the ball by turning my left side to him and that made it tough to see the whole floor.

It meant the guys inside had to work especially hard to find an open passing lane, but I told you, those guys are good and they never stopped moving which made it possible for me to still get the ball to them. Then their coach went to a two-three zone, forcing us to make some outside shots.

Our coach called a time out and shifted us into a motion offense so we could make better screens and cuts off the screens and then the game began to open up. For the first time I got enough room to shoot and after I stuck four three-pointers they dropped the zone and played a kind of box and one with their point guard in my face, trying to deny me the ball.

I never worked so hard for so little. The guy was really good and the only way I could get open was to find Tom or Joe when they came out to set a screen while one of them went to the hole allowing me to pass, or take my shot.

I always prefer to push the ball in low because it's just a whole lot easier to make a basket from a foot than it is from twenty feet. On the inside they couldn't match up with us and I got Walt Marion, our shooting guard, to get his feet in gear and move so that he could get open. Walt can shoot the lights out, but his feet are so slow I think he wears lead shoes.

Meanwhile, everybody in the place was screaming and the weird thing was that I heard it. I never hear the noise, but now I was hearing it and it was getting in my way even though they were cheering for us. And then I went to the hole. Joe set a monster screen and I ran my guy right into him and went airborne and slammed it home. Back on defense, picking up my man, I kept myself low. I may not run very fast but I've got quick feet and hands and when he tried to crossover with his dribble, I slapped it away and took it down court and slammed it home again. And suddenly all I could hear were the basketball shoes squeaking against the wooden floor.

Those two baskets put us up by ten and then Blessington began to come unglued. They made mistakes. Their timing went ragged and then we tightened up our defense and by the middle of the fourth quarter we were up by twenty-four and running away with the game. We could do nothing wrong. Our passing was sharp and crisp and our inside game just ripped the lungs out of them.

I don't know how many times I've heard the saying, "all good things come to an end," but probably way too often. And when the good things ended that night, it happened in a way I never saw coming.

It was on a fast break. I had the ball and I'd forced my way to the center of the floor and I had only one guy to beat and Joe was coming up fast on my left. I waited until he cleared and then I shot him a no-look pass on a single bounce and the guy who was guarding me turned and when he did my foot came down on his foot and my left ankle went over and I went down like I'd been hit with a baseball bat.

Oh, man did that hurt. I yelped like a beaten dog and rolled over several times and then just sat there with my ankle throbbing like the inside of somebody's bass drum. All I wanted to do was swear. It just seemed like the most natural thing to do but somehow I kept my complaints to some low groans.

Through half-shut eyes I saw Joe go up and slam the ball home and then the whistle blew and Coach came running onto the court. He took off my shoe and already the ankle was black and blue and starting to swell and I thought I was looking at the end of my season. It had to be broken. It couldn't possibly hurt that badly and not be broken.

No noise. The gym was so quiet you could've done a commercial for a cellular phone.

"I think it's just sprained, Harley," he said. "But you'll need to see a doctor."

They helped me up and with Joe and Tom on each side I got to the bench and sat down. Then the EMT showed up and looked at the ankle.

"Well, at least it's not life-threatening," she said.

How dumb was that? In the winter, basketball is my life and clearly I was not gonna be playing for some time, so it was definitely life-threatening.

Then Mom and Dad and Janey came down out of the bleachers, and it was off to the emergency room for X-rays and a lot of twisting and pulling that I resented greatly, but only because of the pain. What is it with those medical people? Are they some kind of sadists? Man, oh man, did that hurt. A couple of times I thought I'd pass out. I hate pain. Everybody hates pain. It gets in the way.

They gave me something for the pain, wrapped the ankle and sent me home with all sorts of instructions, none of which I could remember. Good thing my parents were there.

The one thing I did remember was the doctor saying it wasn't broken and that I was lucky it was a low ankle sprain and I'd have to take it easy for several weeks.

SEVERAL WEEKS! It was like the end of the world. Yeah, well, I thought maybe it wouldn't be that long. I'd just get coach to tape it up and I could go. I knew I could. Until I tried to walk. I couldn't put any weight on it at all and I had to use crutches and as far as I was concerned there was nothing but dismal, doleful dark at the end of the tunnel.

But when we pulled into the driveway, there was Soc in his big truck. He climbed out and walked over to us and I introduced him to my folks who were pretty impressed that he turned up when I was hurt. Hey, I was impressed and then I thought that if it'd been him, I'd have been there too. That's what friends do, right?

Well, I got inside and onto the couch in the den and Soc followed Mom out to the kitchen and came back with a couple of Cokes and sat down on the chair across from me.

"What's the doc say?" he asked.

"Several weeks."

"But it's not broken."

"Just a sprain."

He shook his head. "Well, that still pretty much sucks."

"Like totally," I said.

He grinned. "Naw, not totally. Totally would be having a big knife sticking out of your chest."

For the first time I managed a smile. "Yeah, that's totally."

"That guy we picked up never went into the Waterside. We dropped him off and that's the last anyone saw of him."

"So what do they figure? That he hijacked the guy in the Mercedes and then stopped us to get a ride?"

"Something like that."

"Guy's got guts, huh?"

"Absolute brass."

"It's the same guy," I said.

"You think so?"

"Yeah, it is," I said. "The other guy I saw had the same kind of knife stuck in him. And this is no ordinary kind of knife. It's like one of those fantasy knives and the handle has a big snarling head on it. And the guy we picked up was wearing the same baseball cap I saw the first time."

"You're sure about the hat?"

"Absolutely. No logo of any kind and the edge of the brim is red and the whole thing looks like it got run over by the eastbound stage."

Soc laughed. "The eastbound stage, huh? You sure it wasn't the westbound stage?"

"No, definitely eastbound. And John Wayne was driving, with Chill Wills riding shotgun."

We both laughed and I was beginning to feel a whole lot better. And then I moved my leg and the ankle let me know that it wasn't happy, and I grimaced.

"I busted my leg once," Soc said.

"That must've hurt."

"Well, it did and I can't deny it. I was in a cast for six weeks and when they took the cast off I could hardly walk my leg was so shriveled."

"Is that supposed to cheer me up?"

"Sure. You won't have as far to go to rehab it."

"I'm still looking at missing eight to ten games."

"Maybe, maybe not. I guess it depends on how fast you heal."

"Do you know that? Nobody knows that."

"Right. So that means that whatever the doctor told you

could be wrong."

"But he could also be wrong in the other direction."

"You'd know if he was."

"How would I know that?" I asked.

"He'd have told you if it was gonna take much longer, I think."

Well, that brightened me up considerably. "Maybe you're right."

"Always right," Soc said. "Except in English. Is anyone ever right in English?"

"Girls," I said.

"That's true, isn't it?"

"I think so."

"Me too." He shook his head, finished his soda and stood up. "I gotta go. Big day tomorrow. Dad and I have to put a new engine in one of the trucks."

"A whole new engine?"

"We were hoping to get through the winter with it but this last storm pretty much did it in."

"You know how to put an engine in?"

"Sure."

"That is awesome."

"But not like those passes you made tonight. Now that was awesome. Not to mention the way you shoot. How do you do that with someone waving his hands in your face?"

"I never see him. All I see is the rim."

"Concentration."

"Focus." He grinned. "You gonna enter the pool tournament?"

"Already signed up."

"Shouldn't be too hard on the ankle."

"It's a sport. All sports start with the feet. And in pool the way you set your feet controls your angle on the ball. I'm gonna need both wheels."

"Who'd have thought, huh?"

"My dad. He used to win all kinds of tournaments."

"They can be pretty useful."

"What?"

"Dads. They know stuff."

I wondered where he was going with that but with Soc you never knew.

"Saw you talking to April the other day."

"She seems really nice."

"She is. We grew up together ... but she kept on growing when everybody else stopped." Soc shook his head. "I haven't talked to her in a long time."

"I'm thinking of asking her out."

"How tall is she?"

"Six-two."

"So, even with a rangy guy like you she couldn't wear heels."

I laughed. "Never thought about it," I said.

"Well, think about this. I think we can nail the killer."

"What?"

"You interested?"

"No! I mean, maybe! I mean, I don't know anything about guys like that and I'm not exactly bristling with weapons, as you may have noticed."

"It won't be like that."

"What makes you think we can do this?"

He grinned. "I know some things. I'll tell you about it tomorrow ... after we get the engine in. They're calling for snow. So that comes first."

"More snow?"

"Don't you love it? We're gonna make a ton of money if this keeps up."

I grinned. "And they'll postpone and reschedule the games so I won't miss as many as I thought."

"So in this matter of snow we're on the same side."

"Never in doubt," I said.

"You wanna come along again?"

"Sure."

"Your ankle strong enough?"

"I can sit there as well as here." Suddenly the images of big knives sticking out of people popped into my head. "I don't know, Soc, are you sure about this?"

"About what?"

"Trying to catch this guy."

"We won't really catch him. All we'll do is gather information and put it together and give it to Nick."

"Why would we do it any better than the police?"

"Because we're both pretty smart guys. And there's no pressure on us to solve it. Nick's getting a lot of heat now and even the State Police are in on it. He even thinks the FBI may be getting into it."

"I don't know anything about catching killers. Do you?"

"Nope."

"But you think we can do it anyway."

"Yup."

One thing I learned about Soc. When he believes he can do something, he can. After all, as far as I knew everybody in school but me thought he was the most bad-ass of all bad-ass dudes and they were wrong. Not something your ordinary citizen can pull off.

And anyway, deep down inside, I was excited. I mean, how often do you get the chance to catch a killer? At the same time I was shaking in my shoes. After all, he knew who we were, but we knew nothing about him. It meant he could get pretty close to us without worrying about being recognized ... as long as he didn't wear that baseball cap.

"You'd know that knife if you saw it?"

"Sure."

"Well, that gives us something to work on."

10 Getting To Know Socrates

More snow. And once more I was riding shotgun and we'd been talking about this and that when I decided I needed to know a lot more about Socrates Keefer. I'm not a subtle guy.

"What's the Snake thing really all about?"

He laughed. "I told you. It keeps the bullies away."

"Except that I don't see you as the kind of a guy who's a target."

"But I was when I started. I didn't even grow until last year. I also hate getting into fights. I went through that in grammar school. This is a kind of a tough town. I mean, at one end, it's mostly working class families and at the other end it's gotten pretty ritzy. I was always in between."

"So you got picked on."

"Yeah. And then Dad brought home a movie called "The Wild One" with Marlon Brando as the head of this motorcycle gang. That's where I got the idea for the leather. For some reason guys who wear leather are considered tough. Not just any leather, but biker leather."

"And they backed off."

"The bullies all come from the blue collar end of town, except for a few hockey and football guys. It wasn't so much that they backed off, as they didn't seem to notice me. It was like I was wearing camouflage. At the same time the kids from the ritzy end of town stopped talking to me. They wouldn't even look at me! Finally, I think they stopped seeing me altogether."

"Even your friends?"

"The truth is, I didn't have many friends. I got high grades so one crowd had nothing to do with me, except as someone to pick on. The upscale kids thought of me as competition, I think. But part of that may have been Dad's business. They saw him as a guy who mowed lawns and plowed snow. A working man and nothing more and that's the way they saw me. The thing is, we make a lot of money and my family on both sides goes back to the sixteen hundreds, but the upscale yuppies don't seem to be in touch with any of that.

"And they all go to some church or another and we don't. Dad and Mom gave it up after their last argument with the minister at the First Congregational. The Board of Deacons didn't much care for Dad's outspokenness and they were glad to see us go until the treasurer told them how much money went with us. Then they tried to weasel us into coming back but Dad was through with them. His family founded that church, but nobody seemed to know that. What it came down to was another strike against us." He laughed. "Until those same people need plants for landscaping or they hire an architect to do their grounds and we do all the work and supply all the plants and cash their checks."

"But why do you still keep up the front?"

He turned the plow into another driveway and he stopped talking until he had cleared it.

"You fall into things. I mean, you find yourself having done stuff that's pretty much on the edge but then you discover that suddenly things are going smoother. Nobody hassles me. Nobody picks on me. So I go with the flow."

He dropped the plow and slashed into the next driveway, sending the light fluffy snow flying to the right and then he cut the plow, made a sweep past the three-bay garage, backed around, and swept the paved area clear and then used the back of the plow to clear away the berm in front of the garage doors and made one final sweep to the street to widen the driveway.

He was fast and efficient, no wasted energy.

"What about the rumors, the stories about you? Who started that?"

"I did. I dropped hints, left notes where they'd be found. I sneered a lot. The clothes helped. Mostly I stopped talking."

"What did your parents say about that?"

"I got a mountain of crap. But I kept my grades high and I worked hard and I saved my money so I could buy my Harley. Dad didn't worry about it much, but my mother puts more emphasis on social stuff so she was pretty upset. She still is. She's on my case all the time about flunking gym because she wants my name in the paper when they print the honors lists." He shrugged. "I guess if I were my kid, I'd want that to show."

"Makes sense. Parents want to be proud of their kids."

"I tell her not to worry. The colleges will look at my grades and they'll pay no attention to the gym. I have to pass it the next two terms though, or they won't let me graduate." He shook his head. "Maybe I'll join the golf team this spring."

"Which is, of course, all upscale guys."

"Exactly."

"Can you make it?"

He laughed. "I'm a four handicapper and the best they've got is Paul Young who's an eight. It's a dunk shot."

I didn't think I had ever met a guy with more confidence. But the thing was, I already knew he could back it up. I smiled to myself. I wasn't exactly shy in the confidence department either and I thought that might explain why we got along.

"And I suppose you hammered the PSAT's, right?"

"I took the SAT's last spring when everyone else was taking the PSAT's." He glanced around at me. "Fifteen-sixty.

And I haven't even talked to the golf coaches yet."

"So what are you looking at? Yale? Harvard?"

"They're on my list. What about you?"

"Bowdoin. It's a family thing. My brother's there now."

"So. A first-rate school."

"Yeah."

"And you get to play basketball."

"I think so."

"Got any more questions?" he asked.

"Maybe," I said.

"Do you need the answers?"

"I'm not sure I do."

"That's a good sign, Harley."

For awhile, in a neighborhood where the houses were close, Soc plowed snow and I listened to country music. Then we headed out into the part of town where there were far fewer houses and the next thing I knew we were cruising down the road where we'd seen the last victim and that started the next round of conversation.

I'd spent a lot of my time talking to the guys I played basketball with and most of those conversations were not what you'd call discussions unless the subject was sports. But with Soc, that was definitely not the case. He liked to think and he expected me to think, which wasn't something I'd ever been expected to do out loud.

"So what's your guess on our serial killer?" he asked.

"Serial killer? Who's saying that?"

"Nobody yet. But that's what he is. The cops don't want to say that because it scares people."

"Well, sure," I said. "Scares me, and I'm fearless."

He grinned. "Got any ideas?"

"On what?"

"On who it might be."

"You'd know that better than I would," I said.

"Because I've lived here all my life."

"Sure."

"But that can blind you. Whereas, you, coming from away, you might see things I don't 'cause I've seen them all my life."

"You get used to them."

"Exactly."

"We still see them but we don't react to them. I think that the first time we see something, we put it in a category. We do that by making assumptions and sometimes the assumptions are wrong. We saw a guy whose car had gone off the road in a snowstorm and we made an assumption that there was nothing more to it. Now, I wonder what our assumptions didn't allow us to see that would have made us suspicious."

"Big question."

"Huge."

"Maybe not answerable."

"Maybe not."

"Let's try something else, " I said.

"Sure."

"Can you think of anyone in town who might start killing people?"

"I've been doing just that. In fact, I made a list." He reached into his shirt pocket, took out a folded piece of paper and handed it to me. "The names might not mean much."

"Probably not." I looked at the list. Five names. "But if the killer is any one of these guys wouldn't you have recognized him when he climbed into the truck?"

"You remember what I just said about assumptions? I had it in my mind that this was just a guy who had run off the road. I never really looked at him beyond his top coat and noting that it didn't go with his baseball cap. But it was snowing hard and I figured he probably didn't have a dress hat so he used what he had."

"Sounds logical."

"But it wasn't. There was no logic required to reach that decision because it was automatic. I never really thought about the conclusion I reached."

"How well do you know the men on this list?"

"I've seen them around but I don't think I've ever talked to any of them. But remember, I've lived here all my life. Things get said about people and if you hear that often enough, you begin to believe it's true. Could I pick these guys out of a crowd? Sure. Could I identify them by the sound of their voices? Not a chance."

"Then how did you pick them?"

He shrugged. "Not sure. Maybe I don't even know. It was what came up when I asked the question."

"You want to go through this and explain why they made your list?"

"Okay."

"C.B. Renkler."

"Also known as Roadkill Renkler. He lives alone in the old family house. He's about forty-five or so, keeps a really nasty German Shepherd, works for the town crew as a truck driver. He hunts and fishes mostly. He's got an eighteen foot boat that he keeps at a marina on the river. He shaves about once a month, never seems to take a bath. He eats only what he kills, or so I've heard. But nobody has ever seen him buying groceries. In the winter he drives one of the town plows. He's good at it. He works hard."

"And he really eats roadkills?"

"So they say."

"Okay. A weird guy. But why would he kill people?"

"Years ago, maybe ten years ago, or so the story goes, he got into a fight with a guy in a bar. He's a big man and the guy threw a punch at him and Renkler punched him back and the guy fell and broke his neck. They tried him for manslaughter but his lawyer pleaded self-defense and got him off. After that he stopped going to bars or to any public place.

"Then one night somebody beat up his father. The guy was in the hospital for a month and when he got out he disappeared. So did Roadkill. His mother lived alone in the house and worked as a waitress at the Waterside. Then, about a year or so later, she was diagnosed with cancer, and C.B. came home and took care of her till she died. The father was never heard from again."

"Still, Soc, just weird."

"There's more. Three summers ago he was out fishing on the river and some drunks in a big power boat decided to run some waves at him. They circled his boat at nearly full power until they had him rocking on his beam ends. He just sat there and waited and finally they went away. But he recognized them and later, back at the marina somebody beat the crap out of all four of 'em. Put two of 'em in the hospital for about a week. Broken jaws, broken noses, ribs, you name it. They couldn't identify their assailant. It all happened too fast and they were still drunk."

"So how do you know it was Renkler?"

"He's the only guy I know of who could've done it and several people saw those guys harassing him on the water. And then, at work, one of the guys noticed that his knuckles were badly bruised."

"But it would take something to set him off. In both cases he was defending himself, right?"

"You're right. Absolutely."

"Next name," I said. "John Cuccinello."

"He runs the comic book store and lives alone in an apartment upstairs. When you walk into the store, at first it just looks like a comics store, but then after a while you notice that only the comics with the most violent covers are on display in the front of the store."

"I've never been in there."

"Take a look sometime. And then see if you can get Little John into a conversation about some particular comic."

"Little John?"

"Everybody calls him that, but not to his face. It's from Robin Hood. The fat friar?" He laughed. "John's pretty round but he's also taller than you are. Sometimes he wears monk robes and carries a big staff."

"Well, that's pretty much over the top."

"Way, way over. But that's not the reason I chose him. He also sells knives, very expensive handmade knives, mostly, but he also has a section of commercially made knives. Get him talking about the knives and watch his face."

I laughed. "And we've only gotten through two so far. What kind of a town is this?"

"Perfectly normal. Every town has people like this."

He looked into his mirror and then back up at the driveway ahead. He flipped on his blinker and slowed but though the road had been plowed the car stayed behind us.

"Com'on, you idiot, pass me," Soc said into the rearview mirror.

The car stayed behind.

"Okay then," Soc said, "you can wait." Five minutes later he turned the wheel and pushed away the berm left by the town plow, then swung into the driveway. It was a long drive, that wound up over a low rise, then dipped into a swale and finally ran through a double row of big old maples up to the house. There was a lot to plow, the circular drive in front of the house and then the drive out to the garages and the huge turnaround area and finally back out to the road.

The car was gone and Soc turned to the left and headed for the next plowing job about a mile away.

Halfway there Soc looked into his mirror at a car speeding up behind us. I looked back and I couldn't believe anyone would drive that fast over snowy roads.

"What the ... is he chasing us?" I asked.

"I don't know, but get ready."

"Ready? How do I get ready? What do I get ready for?"

"Hang onto something."

There wasn't anything to hang onto except the seat belt and I wrapped my hands around that and watched the car coming closer and closer, the lights on high beam.

"What are we looking at here?" I asked.

"Just hang on."

The car pulled out into the oncoming lane and pulled up

alongside and I heard it backfire and then Soc cut the wheel to the left and drove the edge of the plow into the car. That was all it took to break the traction and the car began to spin end for end.

"Damn!" I shouted, hanging on to the seat belt as if it were a lifeline.

Even with four-wheel drive Soc had trouble bringing the truck under control. He did it by using the gas and not the brakes, each time accelerating out of the skid until we were once again headed straight.

"Where is he?" Soc asked.

"A hundred yards back. The only thing that kept him on the road was the plow berm."

"Is he stopped?"

"He's going away, fast."

"Just as well." He picked up the cell phone and called the base.

"Mom, you're not gonna believe this but some guy just took a shot at me. He's driving a black Ford Taurus headed East on Hingman Road. I put the plow into his right front fender and it's pretty-well gashed up. Yeah, okay. I'll meet them at Warner's. I should just have time to get that one done before they get here."

Talk about a cool customer. I'm shaking in my shoes and he's thinking about knocking off another driveway before the cops get there. That's when I began to think that the leather clothes had nothing to do with why people had decided to leave Soc alone. They saw something else, some internal beast they didn't wish to rouse. And now, seeing it first hand, it was making me more than a little uneasy.

I was a whole lot more than uneasy when we stopped at the end of the Warner's driveway and looked at the bullet hole through the bottom of the door on his side and the bottom of the door on my side. The thing had gone right through the truck and right under our butts. Something like that, I thought, could make you nervous about ever sitting down again.

11 Riding Shotgun

After we got through with the cops we headed back to base to refuel. I had been thinking that maybe we'd quit for the night. It seemed logical that after having somebody shoot a hole through your truck, you might want to lie low for awhile, but Soc had a different idea. He went into the house and came back out lugging a gun case and a box of ammunition.

He opened the back door, unzipped the case, loaded several rounds into the magazine, let the bolt fly forward to chamber a round, and then checked to make sure the safety was on. Finally, he slipped the gun into the case and set it on the back seat with the case unzipped.

He noticed my astonishment. How could he miss. My mouth looked like I was getting ready to swallow something about the size of your average buffalo and my eyes must have been at least the size of a giant squid.

"Your parents let you do that?"

"Dad's plowing and Mom's working the phones and the radio."

"So they don't know."

He shrugged. "They know what happened and that I'm going back out to plow." He pointed upward into the sky. "It's still coming down and I've got a lot of driveways to plow. The good news is that we'll only have to do them once. The storm's got about an hour more to run and it's already tapering off." He stood outside the cab looking at me as he waited for the tank to fill. "If you're nervous about the gun I can drop you off at your house."

"No. It's okay. I don't know anything about 'em, that's all. My mother's not big on guns."

"We won't need it. Whoever he is, he won't be back tonight. He's got half the cops in this end of the state looking for him. And because of the storm, there're so few cars on the road, he'll be pretty easy to spot."

The fuel pump shut off and he hung up the nozzle and climbed up into the cab, bringing the smell of diesel fuel with him.

"Pretty exciting night, huh? Bet you don't get to do good stuff like this all the time."

"Hardly ever," I said.

He closed the truck door, and we headed out. He was right about the snow. It wasn't falling nearly as hard and we made good time as we headed across town to pick up where we'd left off.

"You probably think I'm crazy, right?"

"Yeah, well, maybe not crazy, but abnormal sure as heck crossed my mind," I said.

"That's good. I like that. Normal sucks."

"Hey, everything in its place, you know?"

"For everything there is a season and a time for every purpose under Heaven."

"I know that. Ecclesiastes."

"Interesting dude."

"Like, better a live dog than a dead lion."

"That too." He laughed. "I think you're really pretty worried about all this, aren't you?"

"Who me? Naw. All in a day's work, plow snow, take a round through the cab ... nothing to it."

"I'm kinda hoping he'll make another pass at us, 'cause now, I've got the equalizer."

"You'd shoot him? You'd really do that?"

"Certain. Absolutely certain. That shotgun is a Benelli. It's a semi-auto and it carries eight rounds. Right now it's loaded with alternating rounds of double-ought buck and BB's. Very nasty. You don't even have to aim. The gun recycles so fast that you can almost fill the air with lead just by sweeping the barrel and pulling the trigger."

"Why would you have a gun like that?"

"It's my duck gun."

"What?"

"Plug the magazine so it only takes two rounds and it's legal for waterfowl. It's even got a camo finish."

"I'm kind of confused here, I ..." He was looking into the outside mirror.

"You see something?"

"Another truck, that's all. Keep an eye on him. Tell me if he does anything strange."

"What am I looking for here? Maybe a Gatling gun mounted on his hood?"

"Harley, you're beginning to get the hang of this."

"Just as long as I don't get hung *for* it."

"We aren't breaking too many laws here. The gun is legal because I've got a hunting license. Having it loaded in the cab is kind of on the wrong side of the law, but carrying it around unloaded wouldn't be much help. Besides nobody is going to stop us. Even if they did, it's a pretty good bet they'd look the other way. And anyway, we'd have time to unload before we stopped."

I felt like I was maybe on Mars. My mother's totally against guns, though, now that I thought about it, I wasn't sure where Dad stood on that. But I was absolutely certain that if they knew what I was doing, they'd go postal. Well, maybe not postal, because to do that you have to have a gun, but they would not be happy campers. I looked back at the truck.

"Any change?" Soc asked.

"No."

"Good. Shoot-outs definitely cut into my snow plowing time and I've got half my list to go. I figure after we do the rest of the places out in horse country, I'll drop you off so you can get some rest. Can't have that ankle swelling up."

"That truck is moving up on us."

"We're gonna turn right up ahead. We'll see what he does." He put on the blinker and slowed and the pickup came up behind us, but he waited until we turned, rather than swinging out into the oncoming lane. He even tapped his horn as he went by and Soc tapped his horn in return.

"That was Walter Pinkus. I thought it might be him. He bashed in his right fender a while ago and the headlight on that side is kind of askew."

"Why would he be out in the storm?"

"Walter has a little drinking problem so he never keeps any whiskey at home."

"Which makes him a sort of perpetually drunk driver?"

"He'll stop up ahead at the River Rat, have two drinks and go home. Guy like Walter, two drinks do nothing more than give him a little buzz. He's a big guy. Must weigh close to three hundred. I think all the fat just absorbs the booze."

"There's a whole world out here that I know nothing about."

"Most people don't. And none of the new people. Things

are more private in the dark."

"When people are home watching TV."

"Yeah. Home watching TV."

"And we're out here with the boozers and the lead-slingers."

"Cool, huh? Who else gets to have this kind of fun?"

He was getting to me. It was fun. It was the most exciting thing that had ever happened to me. I was even thinking that I ought to learn about guns and I was sure as heck thinking that I needed a Harley.

I saw it out of the corner of my eye, parked in a turn around in one of the long driveways we had already plowed.

"Whoa, stop! I saw the car!"

Soc stopped, but slowly, and then backed up and turned up into the drive and stopped. In the lights we could see the black Taurus. He reached into the back seat, unlimbered the shotgun, and handed it to me.

My stomach felt like I'd swallowed a bunch of busy little animals.

"Just hold it. I'm going to pull up and then shut off the lights and walk up on the car."

"What if he's in there?"

"That's why I'm shutting off the lights. I'll use the truck for cover and then I'll step into the woods."

"Why don't you just call the cops?"

"No fun in that," he said and he put the truck in gear

and pulled slowly up behind the car with the lights off. It gave our eyes a chance to adjust to the dark, which because of the snow on the ground wasn't all that dark.

"When I get out you keep a watch. If you see anything move, then turn on the truck lights." He pointed to two pull switches.

"Okay." I handed him the shotgun.

He flicked the cab light to the off position so it wouldn't go on when he opened the door, then slipped out and off into the woods. I waited, staring out the front, looking for the least movement. But it was absolutely still and the next thing I saw was a light come on and sweep the inside of the car and then Soc walked back to the truck.

He opened the door and turned on the lights. That was when I noticed the little flashlight mounted under the barrel of the shotgun, which I somehow had missed seeing before. "What's that light all about?"

"It's a tac light, tac for tactical. It lights up the target."

"Whoa ..." I was impressed.

"If your ankle is strong enough you can go take a look. It'll make it three out of four."

"There's another one?"

He climbed into the cab and picked up the phone, punched in the number, and started the engine.

"We keep this up," he said, "and the cops are gonna start suspecting us."

"Who? A gimped-up point guard and a guy who carries a duck gun with a tac light on it?"

"Very handy, that light," he said. "Ducks fly into a dark barn, you got 'em."

I laughed, slid down out of the truck, and worked my way through the snow to the car and shone the light through the window, staring at the brass head and the leather wrapped handle of the knife as a shiver danced down my spine. I shone the light on the guy's face and I knew without a doubt that I had seen him somewhere. Then it hit me. I had seen all of them when they were alive.

But how could that be? Where did I ever go? It had to be my imagination, though to tell you the truth I'm not the most imaginative guy I know. I tend to stick with facts. And this was a fact. I knew I had seen them but I couldn't think where. To tell you the truth, just then my mind wasn't doing a whole lot of rational work because it was focused on being weirded out.

12 Janey

But despite the fact that I had, in no time at all, gone from never having seen a body even at a funeral to having seen three murder victims, I didn't freak out.

Which meant my family was watching me like I was some kind of test tube experiment, waiting for me to boil over or maybe explode. But nobody talked about it and I guess maybe they were waiting for me to say something.

I didn't. I couldn't.

Maybe it should have made me weird or a little crazy, but somehow my brain had wrapped itself around what I had seen and carefully moved it to a place where I could look at it objectively without my emotions getting loose and running amok, even though that hadn't happened since I was a real little kid.

I guess between the ankle injury and the bodies I should have been a basket case, or at least everybody thought I should have been, and that was why, I think, my sister Janey was so nice, which was pretty different for her. She's thirteen, as I said, and she's an expert at being thirteen. But I remembered being that age and the only thing I could do was be patient and wait for her to grow out of it. I mean, nobody stays thirteen.

But Janey took me by surprise. She got me sodas and she even talked. It was like getting to know someone you had known your whole life and never known at all. But we never talked about the killings, though I'm sure that was high on her list.

Instead, she talked about something else and it pretty much knocked my socks off. She was worried about what boys thought about girls who were athletes.

I took my time answering that one, mostly because I don't think until she asked it, that I'd ever given it any thought. But she needed to know because she was already five-ten and growing and there were only two guys in her class who were taller.

She took my hesitation as a negative. "They don't like them, do they."

Did I tell you she's pretty? Maybe I didn't. But I'm not sure until then I ever thought of her as pretty or not. She'd always been just my annoying little sister. Talk about a wake-up call.

"I never thought about it, Janey. And I never heard any

guy say anything about it."

"But they don't ask them out, do they?"

"I have to think about it. I mean, it's not something I ever kept track of."

"They ask out the cheerleaders."

It was getting worse by the second. "Give me a break here, little sister. We've switched schools so often that it's hard to remember. All I can say is that it doesn't make any difference to me. I like tall girls and the basketball team is where a lot of them turn up." And then I smiled as I thought about talking with April Dunhill, the starting center on the girls' team. "One of the things I like is that we always have something in common to talk about."

She smiled. "That's cool," she said. "Most guys never have anything to say."

I laughed. "And the girls never stop talking."

"We do too." She feigned indignation.

"Maybe it's a guy-girl thing," I said. "When they're nervous, guys usually shut up and girls usually talk. Does that make sense?"

She was admitting nothing. "Maybe."

"Look," I said, "don't worry about it. Play basketball and enjoy it. Don't worry about the other stuff. It works out. I think sometimes guys who aren't athletes are kind of scared of girls who are good at sports."

I didn't see her next question coming either.

"Most of the jocks aren't very interesting," she said.

"Because all they think about is sports."

"Something like that."

"They have to if they're gonna be good."

"You don't."

"But I'm not going Division One either. I can probably play Division Three college ball but when it comes to Division One I'm riding the bench. And anyway, you remember last summer? How many hours did I spend out on the court?"

"A lot." She rolled her eyes. "All you did was play basketball and shoot pool."

"Which makes me a pretty boring guy, right?"

"But you don't talk about sports."

That was something else I'd never thought about. But it was true. I mean, what was the point of rehashing games that had been played ... well there was a point ... I was sure of it but I couldn't pin it down. I couldn't remember ever talking about a game at home.

"What do girls talk about?"

"Nothing much."

Evasion.

"Boys?"

"Sure."

"And because you're so tall, you don't have as many to talk about."

"I don't think I'm getting all of this," she said.

I laughed. "Yeah," I said, "right. I think you got it all. Your problem is that your height has kind of narrowed the field."

She blushed. "How did you guess that?"

"I'm smart."

"Well, nobody ever doubted that. Everybody in this family is smart."

"Janey, what it comes down to is that sports are games. And for most of us that's all they'll ever be. But that's okay because if we work hard at them we get to play, maybe even star for a while. For guys, to go beyond that, you have to be an awesome athlete. But girls get a better chance to play at the top level because there are fewer girls who are willing to push their ability. And now I'm guessing that was behind what you were asking, isn't it?"

"Yeah."

"Well, here's what it comes down to. How badly do you want to play basketball?"

"A lot, Harley. A whole lot. I just don't want to give up everything else."

"Meaning boys."

"Well ...duh ..."

I laughed. "Hey, You don't have to give up anything."

"Sure, and when it comes to proms and stuff, who's gonna ask an Amazon?"

"You know who I'm asking to the prom?"

"Who?" She lit up like a Christmas tree. This was a sub-ject she could really get her teeth into.

"You can't say anything because I haven't asked her yet."

"OhmyGod, who, Harley?"

"April Dunhill."

"She's gorgeous!"

"Think I've got a chance?"

"She's really, really nice, Harley. She coaches my team in the Saturday league. I like her a lot."

"Well, that's all the recommendation I need."

"You'd take my recommendation?" She *never* saw that coming.

"I just hope she'll go with me."

"I know she will!"

"Do you know something I don't know?"

"I just think she'll say yes."

She said it too quickly.

"Don't look at me that way," she said. "You know girls talk about boys."

"Okay, I won't ask."

"Call her."

That built my courage some, but I didn't rush to the tele-phone. It doesn't work that way.

Every day I went to practice and sat on the bench and helped Earl Jones who was just a freshman and the guy who was going to fill in for me. He's young and still growing but he was already nearly six feet tall and he had great ups.

All he needed was to relax and let the game come to him, keep his head up and see the court. I think if he'd been a junior he'd have been starting at point because he already had game and all he needed was the confidence that would let him take control because, hey, the point guard controls the game.

We worked on that. I kept it clear and simple and got him to believe in his ability to run things. Well, maybe not entirely, because when you're fourteen that's tough to do when you're looking at a floor full of seniors and juniors but bit by bit you could see him gaining confidence.

By Thursday the pain had pretty much gone and I could put some weight on my foot. The ankle was hardly swollen but still, when I had to move around the house, I used the crutches.

Coach checked out the ankle after practice. "This may not be as serious as I first thought."

"The doctor told me several weeks," I said.

"Well, Harley, I'm gonna bet that I've seen more ankle sprains than most any doc and it looks to me like you're a real fast healer. I think you'll be back on the court in a week. You won't be able to go full speed, but we'll tape you up and at least you can get some work in so you don't go stale." He picked up the elastic bandage and rewrapped the ankle. "I'm thinking two weeks and you'll be playing. We've only got two games to go before Christmas break and by the time we get into January you should be fine." He stood up. "Plenty of tape, though. You'll still need it taped before practice and games so you don't twist it again."

"Thanks, Coach," I said. "I hate missing practice as much as the games."

"The important thing is to give it complete rest."

Here's the thing about being injured. All the stuff you never thought twice about doing, you suddenly can't do.

The snow started to fall about eight that night, just a bunch of fat fluffy flakes at first and then it changed to the fine tiny crystals that began to swirl in the rising wind. For awhile I sat looking out the window, watching it snow.

My cell phone rang and it was Soc.

"Hey, big guy, how's the ankle?"

"Better," I said. "A lot better."

"Good enough to go plowing?"

"Sure."

"If it keeps up, I'll be going out about seven."

"How much are they saying?"

"Six, maybe seven inches."

"That doesn't sound too bad."

"Hey, just enough to have to plow."

"The way I hear it, you guys plow when it flurries."

"Only for those who call us. Otherwise we don't start

until there's four inches on the ground."

"You think we can avoid finding another body?"

He laughed. "You've already seen more than most people see in a lifetime."

"Yeah, but I seem to be getting better at it."

"Hey, everybody's got to be good at something."

"Like acting, huh?"

"Ooooo ... Snap!" He laughed. "See you at seven."

"Okay. Seven it is."

"And, Harley, just so you know. I'm bringing my shot-gun."

"That's okay."

"Be best if you didn't say anything about it, you know?"

"Sure."

"You're sure you're okay with that?"

"Hey, it's cool, Soc. But maybe you better show me how to load and unload it in case we get stopped and you're driving."

"See you in a while."

"Yeah."

I'm not gonna lie to you. That shotgun made me pretty nervous. All I knew about guns is that my parents opposed anyone having a gun except the police and the military.

But here's the way I saw it. If you've got somebody taking potshots at you, then you better have something to shoot back with or you stand a pretty good chance of winding up dead. It was a matter of self-defense, nothing else. No different than basketball. At some point you switch from defense to offense and make your opponent pay. If you don't, you lose.

As true as that was, I didn't know whether I could actually shoot someone. But from what I had always heard, no one knows that until the time comes.

13 Info From The Net

I missed practice on Monday so I could get the ankle checked. Mom picked me up at school at noon because my folks wouldn't let me drive even though it was my left ankle I'd sprained and my car has an automatic transmission.

They told me it had to do with my insurance and I just went along. Some things you don't fight because they aren't worth fighting about and anyway, I was long past being embarrassed by having my parents cart me to school.

"How's the ankle?" Mom asked.

"It doesn't hurt when I walk on it." I tucked the crutches into the back seat and climbed into the front.

"I think you're like your father. I never saw anyone heal as fast as he does."

"All I need is some tape and I could play now."

"When Dr. Thomas says it's okay, you can play."

The appointment wasn't until four and I decided to spend

some time surfing the Net. I punched in "serial killers" and, man, you just never know what's gonna come up on the Net.

I ended up at a site with a long list of serial killings and right near the top was good old Yellow Springs.

> YELLOW SPRINGS — Police have no leads in the killings which started here roughly a month ago. So far four adult males have been killed, each left with a large knife protruding from the body, police said.
>
> In each case the knife had been driven directly through the heart. According to police, the knives are identical, each with an eight-inch blade, and a hilt between the handle and the blade. Each knife also has a leather-wrapped handle and a brass image on the end of the handle.
>
> At first, police said they thought the killings were drug-related, but all four victims were businessmen in the area on sales calls.
>
> The last two were apparently hijacked in their cars, police said.

Most of that had been in the newspaper and on the television, which, Dad says, takes most of its news from the newspapers, but I hadn't seen anything before about hijacking.

I printed it out and went on surfing, looking for any report of serial killings which were similar.

I'd always thought that serial killers were kind of rare, but you wouldn't believe how long that list ran. Of course, a lot of the killings had happened in the past and the killers had been caught, but a surprising number of the cases had not been solved.

I kept plugging away, reading every one, even the killings that had occurred years and years before. Okay, so I'm kind of odd. But I like gathering information. I like knowing things. Hey, knowledge is power, right? You collect enough stuff and nobody can beat you at Trivial Pursuit.

After an hour or so I was getting a little brain weary and I almost missed the story about a series of killings that had occurred back about ten years ago in Colorado in a town called … are you ready for this? Black Springs. How weird is that? Both places are named for springs and only the color was different.

Okay, a little thin, maybe, but here's what it said.

> The serial killings in Black Springs, CO remain unsolved after all these years. In all, there were twelve victims, all male, all traveling salesmen. Each victim was found with a large knife sticking from his chest. The case remains open and the Black Springs Sheriff's office is still working to solve the murders, though a spokesman admitted recently that the trail had disappeared a long time ago.
> He theorized that the killings were the work of a vagrant who simply moved on.

Well, didn't that set my brain wheels to grinding. Was it the same guy? Or was it somebody who had read about the killings just as I had, and decided to repeat the pattern?

The way the brain works is by making connections. It's like a computer. You load in data and then you send in a code which retrieves the data and compares it to other data.

But the brain is a whole lot better at that than a computer, in part because computers don't have imagination, so they have to follow logical patterns. Imagination is free to roam.

From the time I got home until we left for the appointment with Dr. Thomas, all my brain did was leap and thrash and dash about, connecting and discarding and connecting again, only to trash the ideas as improbable.

But for that I would have spent the time on my X-Box. It was a very busy time. I almost filled an entire legal pad with ideas, some of which I lined out right away and others I left to look at later, when my mind wasn't in such a pell mell tumbling rush.

All of this was on my mind as I sat on the examining table waiting for Dr. Thomas. It seemed to take a long time, but then waiting for doctors always takes forever. At least there was a *Sports Illustrated* to read while I waited.

Finally, the door opened and Dr. Thomas came in. He's an inch or two shorter than his son Joe.

He grinned. "I'm under orders. Joe says I've got to get you back on the court as soon as possible 'cause you're the only guy who can get him the ball."

I grinned at the compliment. "Joe's a great player," I said. "Division One all the way."

"Well, I'm hoping. I'm hoping for UConn. That's where I went to school and you can see where it got me. But I wasn't the athlete Joe is. Nowhere near."

He pulled up the table extension and unwrapped my ankle, his eyebrows climbing steadily higher as the wrap came off. "This is looking very good," he said. "In fact, it's much better than I expected."

"I can play then?"

"Let me see ..." Very gently he began to manipulate my foot, watching for any sign that I was in pain.

But I felt no pain at all. It felt absolutely normal ... until he turned my foot outward. Then I felt it.

"Harley, I think we ought to have Dr. Partridge look at this just to be certain. He's an orthopedic surgeon and he's the absolute best when it comes to foot and ankle injuries. I want to make sure you didn't chip a bone and his equipment will tell him that. In fact, he can probably tell that just by moving your foot around."

"Surgeon?" I could see my whole season disappearing.

He laughed. "I don't think there will be any need for surgery. Just a precaution. My guess is that if you're properly taped and you don't go full speed for a couple of weeks, you'll be fine. But you'll need to be taped for practice and games. What you don't want to do is re-injure this ankle and especially you don't want to come down on the side of your foot and break a metatarsal bone. And because the ankle is weak that can happen more easily."

He rewrapped the ankle. "I've got a question for you. I hear that you've seen three of the murder victims. What I want to know is whether it's causing you to lose sleep or whether it's affected your appetite."

"Some pretty bad dreams, but that's all."

"Nasty thing to see."

"It kinda sticks in my mind but not all the time."

"If it begins to cause you any problems at all, let me know, will you? Sometimes things like that can get to you."

"Thanks, Dr. Thomas, I appreciate that."

He smiled, and I gotta tell you, I never saw anyone with a warmer smile. "Hey, I've seen you play and I agree with Joe. You've got game, my friend, you have definitely got game. But more to the point, you've got the head for the game. You see the whole floor and nothing seems to rattle you."

Talk about a stunner. I mean, this was coming from a guy who knew. Stuff like that can go to your head like beer, not that I know anything about drinking beer. Who me? Nothing at all.

"All I have to do is get the ball to Joe and it's in the hole and we win."

"He's making his old Dad proud. No doubt about that."

"How tall will he get?" I asked.

"Six-eight or nine."

"So he needs a mid-range jumper."

"He's working on it."

"I can set it up for him then go inside and hit the boards."

"Well, you got the ups for it. Man, I couldn't believe how

high you got when you came off that screen."

He let the table down.

"How's Joe doing with his studies?"

"There's been a decided improvement along those lines." He grinned. "Oh, I get it. You talked to him."

"He's too smart not to have good grades."

"I enrolled him in the Kaplan SAT course," Dr. Thomas said. "He asked me to."

I nodded. "Good."

"What am I missing here?"

"We're getting to be really good friends, that's all."

"But why would you push him into doing this?"

"Where he's going there's a lot of pressure. If he works hard now, he'll get better at studying and he won't have to worry about grades."

"And if he should get hurt, he'll have something to fall back on."

"Something like that."

On Tuesday I went hurling myself along on the crutches and getting a lot of sympathy, which to tell you the truth, I kind of liked, because, after all, everybody likes that sort of thing.

I got to calculus early and Socrates was waiting for me.

"How's the ankle?"

"I gotta see one more Doc and if he clears me, I'm playing."

"All right!"

I pulled the printout from my notebook and handed it to him. "I found this on the Net."

He read it quickly and handed it back.

"This was on the Net?"

"All of it."

"So you think maybe the guy from Black Springs has moved to Yellow Springs?"

"Or it's a copycat killer."

"You think Nick knows about this?"

"We ought to make sure one way or the other."

"I'll let him know." He stared at me for several seconds. "You're okay with our looking into this, aren't you?"

"You know, the last thing we want to do is attract this guy's attention."

"Still …"

"Soc, the guy is crazy, right? And crazy guys can't be figured."

"You're right. It'd be a crazy thing to do."

"Absolutely."

"On the other hand, the idea of trying to find the killer had a certain undeniable appeal. We ought to try."

"We'd be fools not to," Soc said.

14 Getting Into It

On Friday Afternoon, Mom drove me into the city to see Dr. George Partridge. They took several X-rays and, finally I got to see the doctor. He pushed and pulled at my ankle and then shook his head and smiled.

"When did you say you injured it?"

"Last Friday."

"How badly was it swollen?"

I held my hands together as if I were holding a small melon. "About like that."

"Remarkable." He walked over to the pictures he had taken, stared at them for several minutes and then walked back to the examining table. "I see absolutely nothing to worry about here. Your ankle is fine. No bone chips, no other apparent damage. But that's not to say there isn't some danger. Anytime you twist an ankle it's a pretty good bet you'll twist it again. Things stretch out, the tendons need to recover. What that means is that you can play, but you will need to have that ankle taped. I'm going to give you a set of instructions to give to your coach so that he tapes it the right way."

"All right!"

"What position do you play?"

"Point guard."

"Pretty tall for a point guard."

"Not in college."

He grinned. "No, I suppose not anymore. Got a three point shot?"

"Yup."

"Well, Harley," he said, "good luck with your season. It'd be best if you didn't go full speed for a week or so and you might consider not taking it to the hole for a while. You're most likely to re-injure the ankle when you come back down from jumping. Give yourself the weekend and then start on Monday."

I was back! Talk about pumped!

Later, Soc came over and we went up to my room which is out over the garage and we got into the names on Soc's list, sifting all the details we had and trying to make connections. And all the time I had this thing in the back of my mind that wouldn't come clear.

"Did you tell Lt. Colello?"

"He knew all about it," Soc said.

"And?"

"He says it's a dead end."

"Why would he say that?"

"To make sure we don't go poking around."

But it was too late for that.

What we did was take each possible suspect and go down through the list of serial killers to see if anything connected. It took us several hours and by the end we had three, maybe four guys who would bear watching.

"Something's bothering me with this," I said. "I mean, what do we really know about these guys?"

Soc grinned. "Rumors," he said, "nothing but rumors." He stood up and walked across the room and stood by the wood stove. "The thing we need to sort out is which rumors are true."

"Okay, how?"

"Take Warren. He's also called Red Dog because ..."

"Wait a minute. Is this the same Red Dog who hangs out at Shorty's?"

"Yeah. You know him?"

"Well, as it turns out, I do know him. I shot pool down there all summer, remember?"

"Then you know who Blacky Weaver is too."

"Yeah. And a whole bunch of other guys."

"All of 'em tough."

"I guess. I mean, they look tough, but they've never been anything but nice to me and they even calmed a couple of guys down after I took 'em to nine-ball school."

"So, then, you wanna take Red Dog off the list?"

"I don't know enough about him."

Soc shrugged. "Maybe we could watch them."

"Like some kind of private eyes?"

"Sure."

"We are talking a murderer here, right?"

He nodded. "I'm not saying it wouldn't be dangerous."

"How dangerous?"

"Well, a serial killer follows a ritual of some kind. Now, if the guy were just a thief who kills his victims, he'd have no trouble knocking off a witness or two. But I don't think a serial killer would do that because it wouldn't fall into the pattern he's established. I think he'd probably just run off."

"That's just a guess."

"Well, yeah, but ..."

"No guesses. Just thinking, and what I'm thinking is that I'm kind of uncomfortable with the thought of having some big-ass knife sticking through my heart."

"Are you getting cold feet again, Harley?"

"Maybe."

"But wouldn't you like to nail the guy?"

"Sure, but playing detective, I don't know. I play pool and basketball and baseball. Those are my games."

"But how cool would it be if we caught him? Think what people would say!"

"They'd say 'those stupid kids could have gotten themselves killed.' That's what they'd say, and they'd be right!" But I knew, no matter how I sounded, that I was going to get into it because more and more I had the feeling I knew something that no one else knew.

That still didn't make it any easier. I told you, I'm not a fighter. Maybe I'm even kind of cowardly. Or was it that because I had avoided fights for so long that I didn't really know how I would react. I had no such doubts about Soc.

And there was no holding him back. "What about Cuccinello?" he asked. "Have you been into his shop yet?"

I shook my head. "I don't know anything about him except what you told me before."

"Did anything in that strike you as weird?"

"Yeah. I mean, not many guys walk around wearing monk's robes and carrying a staff."

"You oughta see his face when you ask about one of the knives in the display case."

"Maybe the cops should talk to him," I said. "Maybe he sold the knives that were used in the killings."

"Maybe."

"So what else have you got on him?" I asked.

He shrugged. "Nothing. He's pretty weird, but I've got an old maid aunt who collects antique glass and she acts almost the same way once you get her talking about her collection."

"So, just weird and that's probably all."

He nodded, but I could see that he wasn't ready to give up on the idea. In fact, I had the notion that he was going deeper and deeper into it.

I stopped him. I had to. My stomach was unhappy. "Soc, no offense, man, but I'm not sure I can do this."

"That's cool. It's my thing, I can see that." He shook his head. "What's weirding me out is that something inside my head keeps telling me I'm somehow a part of it, that I know something but I can't put the pieces together."

Well, wasn't that just a little on the spooky side because I had been thinking the same thing. But then, he *was* a part of it. After, all, somebody *had* put a bullet through his truck. Did that make me a part of it too? Well, it did because I had seen the killer too and he had no idea how good a look I'd gotten.

"He's watching us, isn't he," I said.

"Seems like."

"Sure. I mean who else would take a shot at us."

He shrugged. "There could be someone else."

"Like who?"

"We don't plow all the driveways in town. There's at least two other guys and one of them used to do a lot more plowing. But he was lousy and unreliable and gradually people switched their business to us."

"A turf war? You're saying the shot at the truck could be

part of a turf war? Like rival gangs fighting over territory?"

"You asked."

"Does your father know this?"

"Sure. And I told Nick too. They're investigating."

"But what about the fact that we found the body in that car."

"I haven't got that worked out yet."

'Wait a minute here. Are you just making this up so the serial killer theory looks better?"

"You mean because it's outside his pattern, a serial killer wouldn't be likely to do something like that."

"Yeah."

He shook his head. "It would be easier, if that were true."

"All right then. Who else have you majorly pissed off? How about those guys at Shorty's this summer?"

"Naw. Guys like that don't come back at you."

"Bullies?"

"Bullies. Over the hill bullies. In school they ruled but the outside world has got guys a lot nastier."

He was sucking me in. It was like I'd fallen into the edge of a big and powerful whirlpool. I could hear myself talking but it wasn't as if it was really me talking. "Okay, the bottom line here is that the shooting incident is not part of the killings."

"Right," he said. "Well, maybe ..."

"Because the real bottom line is, the guy's a killer. He's

used to whacking people. Why would he let possible witnesses walk around free? And wouldn't it be logical, seeing as a body turned up in the car, that the serial killer and the snow plowing guy are the one and the same?"

"Well, maybe that's what he wants us to think."

"That would mean the first guy abandoned the car and then the killer dumped the body into it."

"Harley, I shouldn't have mentioned the snow plowing guy. He drinks too much and he's lazy, but there is nothing the least spooky about him. He used to work for us but Dad let him go because he never got things done and what he did was never right. Then he went out on his own and, at first, because he undercut our prices he got a lot of business. But after one winter those customers came back to us."

"Would a guy like that have taken a shot at you?"

"Maybe if he got drunk enough."

"But a serial killer probably wouldn't be drunk when he was busy murdering people."

"And even if eliminating witnesses doesn't fit the pattern of crossed wires he's got in his head," Soc said, "you're right. He's still a killer. What he'll do is wait. If nothing happens, if no one shows up to ask questions, he'll know we can't identify him. He knows that the cops can't afford to allow a possible suspect to float because he'll kill someone else."

"And nobody is bothering him."

"Yeah. He knows by now that he's not on anyone's list."

"But he's on your list."

"Maybe."

"So you want to check into the people on the list."

"But they can't know it," Soc said. "We have to find a way to nose around without arousing suspicion, first, because it's dangerous and second, because he might quit and what we need is to identify a target and then keep watch.

"And there's another possibility. Maybe he wanted us to see the car so we would find the body in it. Maybe the shot was just a way to get our attention."

"Now, that's an interesting concept."

"I thought so," I said, "and right now I think I need to read up more on the psychology of serial killers." I stood up and walked across the room, rubbing the back of my neck, which is something I do a lot of when I'm thinking.

"A lot of 'em go after people who are alone."

"In this case, salesmen on the road."

"So far all of them have been salesmen."

"Okay ..." I was pacing now, back and forth. "Is there any other connection."

"Start with the most general," Soc said. "Two guys were hijacked. Two were killed outside pizza shops. All of them were stabbed in the heart with the same kind of knife. What else can you think of?"

"They were all short? Is that true? Because it seems true

to me that it's true, but my memory could be off on that."

"I only saw the last two and yeah, I'd say maybe five-four or five."

"I saw three of them and they were all about that height. Can we check up on that?"

"It should be public record."

"Yeah, but will they show it to us?"

"Nick will if my dad asks him. They're golfing buddies."

"Then maybe that's the direction we should go in."

"I'll talk to Dad."

"Parents get pretty weird about a thing like this."

"You mean about kids our age trying to solve murders?"

"Sure."

"Dad's cool."

"That cool? Cool enough to let you take the risk?"

He shrugged. "Maybe not that cool."

"We could lie," I said.

"Lies can work." He grinned.

"I can say I'm just trying to jog my memory, you know, to see if I can make myself remember something. Lt. Colello told me that can happen. Sometimes things come to you later, once you've calmed down."

I dropped back into the big easy chair next to my desk.

"Hey," Soc said, "I just noticed. You got your wheels back."

"I'm cleared to play. All I have to do is make sure the

ankle is properly taped. It doesn't even hurt."

"That's awesome, dude."

"I'm not supposed to take it to the hole yet, but hey, I can live with that. It'll only be a for a few games and we won't be playing the same team twice so they'll be guessing that I can still go past 'em, and they'll still have to play off me. If they test me, then I'll have to go for it, because if I don't then they'll take away my outside game."

He laughed. "That's the same game I play. Always keep 'em guessing."

"Maybe we better remember that."

"When we start checking into this, you mean?"

"Absolutely, dude. The one thing a serial killer depends upon is predictability. In every case, the victims have in some way been predictable."

"No rumors."

"Just the facts, man, just the facts."

15 Games

Always before it seemed to take forever to get from Thanksgiving to Christmas, but in Yellow Springs the time seemed to roar past, in part, I suspect, because our semester final exams came before the vacation.

But there was also a lot going on. Basketball, of course, and the start of the tournament at Shorty's where I had to play a lot of people just to qualify, and of course the fact that we had a serial killer loose which, as you might suspect, had everyone pretty much on edge.

And there was the matter of talking to April about the prom. Now, I'm usually pretty cool about stuff like that. Probably it's from having met so many new kids each year in high school. You get used to sticking your neck out in situations like that, if only because you don't have a lot of time to get to know people.

But for some reason it was different with April. Go figure. But you can't. No guy can figure stuff like that. It's a lot like writing an English paper instead of taking a math exam. Things are kind of up in the air and there are no solid answers that you can get merely by working the numbers.

At lunch, on a Friday before the game, I took a shot at it. I cruised up to the table where she was sitting with Lottie McDonald and Marty Wilson and asked if I could join them.

April smiled. "Sure," she said.

I set my tray on the table and sat down, trying not to look like Mr.-I'm-so-cool-you-can't-possibly-say-no, instead just trying to be a regular guy.

The two other girls were also on the basketball team and I smiled and offered a compliment. "You guys played a heck of a game last night," I said.

They smiled, watching me carefully, making sure I wasn't just tossing a lot of bull, you know, like I was buttering them up the way guys do before they try asking them out. I hate that stuff.

"Hey, I'm serious. You've got an awesome D. I mean, at the start of the second half you just shut 'em down." I wasn't lying. It was absolutely true. They can play. Not the way the guys play but they knew that and they knew I knew it, but I wasn't comparing them to anyone beyond the women's teams they played against. I mean, fair is fair, you know. They don't jump as high, they can't run as fast, but I'll tell you this. They play together and the guys could learn something from that.

"You really are serious," April said.

"Hey, I've got a tall sister, you know."

"Jane is gonna be really good," Marty said.

"Awesome," I said.

"Are you working with her?" April asked.

"If she asks me." April is pretty. Long blond hair, which she wears in a pony tail just about all the time, and she has kind of hazel eyes and a narrow nose and high cheekbones and big dimples when she smiles.

"She thinks you're the best big brother ever," April said.

"She does?" It really caught me by surprise.

"Of course she does," April said.

"That's cool," I said and I meant it, even though it seemed impossible when you consider all the fights and spats we'd had in the past.

"How's the ankle?" April asked.

"I'm cleared to play but it'll be a while before I can go full speed."

"You gonna play tonight?"

"Yup."

"That's amazing," Lottie said. "When you went down I was sure you were through for the year."

"Me too," I said. "Got lucky."

"You think you guys have a chance at the championship this year?" Marty asked.

I shrugged. "If we all stay healthy and keep playing together."

"My dad says you're gonna make it," Lottie said.

"I wish I knew more about the competition," I said. "All I have to go on is what Coach tells me."

"You've got at least three Division One players," Marty said.

"Okay, Joe, absolutely, Tom, probably, who's the third?"

Suddenly they were all staring at me. "Who? Me? No way. Too slow. There are guys out there who'll eat my lunch."

"Do you really believe that?" April asked.

"Those guys are really fast," I said.

"But most of them are shorter," Marty said.

"Not the guys going D-1. Some of those guards are six-five and six–six."

"You know what our coach says?" April grinned and looked at the other two girls. "Should I tell him?"

"Maybe not," Lottie said. "He won't be able to get his hat on."

I laughed and they laughed with me.

"Okay, I'll tell you." April's smile is devastating. "She tells our guards to watch everything you do on the court and play that way. She says you see the floor and you understand the game better than any high school guard she's ever seen."

"Whoa, what's she been smokin'?" I said.

We all laughed.

"She's serious, Harley," April said. "And she's right. You can have all the athletic ability in the world and not know how to use it, or not be able to get your head into the game." She smiled at her friends. "So the question is, are you just being modest or do you really not know how good you are?"

On the spot. Or at least I should've been. But the truth was, I had always doubted whether I was really any good. I just tried to do what it took to win, to control the game, and get the ball to the people who could score.

"My God," Lottie said. "You really don't know, do you?"

"Well, the thing is, Lottie, I mean, I just do what I do, you know? And I've got great targets with Joe and Tom. Those guys know how to get open. And Keegan is not to be overlooked curling off the screens."

Marty smiled. "That is really cool," she said.

"What's cool?"

Both Lottie and Marty stood and picked up their trays.

"That you think the way you do," April said.

Lottie and Marty walked away and I was left sitting with April. Couldn't have worked out better.

"Would you like to go to the prom with me?"

"Sure," she said. "I'd like that."

Now I was smiling so hard I felt like a circus clown with a smile painted on.

"All right!"

"And I even get to wear heels," she said.

"But not spikes," I said.

"I never wear spikes. I can't walk in 'em, let alone dance." She grinned. "Are you worried that I'd be taller?"

"Of course. I'm not used to girls being taller than I am."

"I think we'll wind up at about the same height."

"Nothing wrong with that."

"Has anybody told you how different you are from most guys?"

Nobody had, but it's one of those things you just sort of know. When you move a lot, you have to find ways to set yourself apart. On the other hand, it seemed to me that I had never acted like other guys. I mean, for some reason, there was just a lot of stuff I didn't worry about.

"Well, you are," she said.

"But not too weird, I hope."

"Not that kind of different. I mean, here we are talking away and we've only talked a couple of times before and there doesn't seem to be a whole lot of stress."

I grinned. I like people who get to the point. "You are truly cool," I said.

"Kind of blunt, though."

"Blunt's fine with me."

"Tell me about the murders," she said.

I looked across the table at her. Well, blunt was okay, but maybe this was a little over the top. "Kind of weird," I said.

"I've seen three of the victims after it happened. Nasty stuff."

"And you've been hanging out with Soc."

I looked at her carefully now, because it was the first time I'd heard anyone in the school but me or Sean use his real name. "I have."

"Some people wonder about that," she said.

"I don't."

"I can see that."

"Does that bother you?"

"He doesn't fool everyone, you know," she said.

"Does a pretty good job though."

"He does. But that's Soc. We've known each other since first grade. Still, it's no wonder you two get along. You both just go your own ways."

"Yeah we do," I said.

"Not many guys are brave enough."

"Or girls," I said.

"When you're a girl and you're over six feet tall, you have no choice but to go your own way."

I heard the peculiar tone in her voice and I understood. "But not a whole lot of fun sometimes, huh?"

"Nope."

"Things improving?"

She smiled at me and she had this flash in her eyes which may have been irony. "As of a few minutes ago," she said.

"Would it surprise you to find out that I feel the same

way?"

"Yup."

"Sometimes," I said, "it's nice to be surprised."

We got up and carried our trays to the counter and I saw Soc and smiled and nodded.

He nodded back. Another curious thing. He always nods up and never down. So did Joe and Tom ... always up. What's with that?

I thought maybe I'd start nodding upward and see what happened.

"Hey, Earth to Harley ..."

"Huh?"

"Your tray," April said.

"Oh, sure." I grinned. "Sorry, I got thinking about something."

She smiled. "I know. You do that a lot."

16   ... And More Games

From the time we started pregame warm-up drills, I knew that my ankle was okay. Not perfect, but okay. I could run easily and I could cut pretty well and I could shoot. But I was not gonna spend a lot of time in the air because when I got too high, I could feel something pull when I came down on the ball of my foot.

The thing is, I was pumped and I had to keep trimming myself to keep from getting too high and forgetting about the ankle.

We usually run. We're big and fast and we'd worked a lot in practice on our transition game, where you go from defense to offense and push the ball up the floor. My job, of course, was to get the ball over the ten-second line and usually I did that by dribbling, but now I passed more, long passes, and nothing moves the ball quicker than a pass.

For several minutes into the game we exchanged baskets and then, when they missed and Joe got the rebound and fired it to me on the wing, I never put the ball on the floor, but lofted a long lead pass to Keegan who had broken for the basket. It hit him right in the hands and he rose up and stuffed home the layup and the kids in the gym erupted in a geyser of noise. There is no sound quite like that when you're out on the floor. It shakes the walls, it makes the floor vibrate. It surrounds you like a thick liquid.

And that's why there is nothing like playing at home. But there is also nothing like making a big play like that early in the game, and while it's even more important when you're playing away because it takes the hometown crowd out of the game, at home it brings down the house and players feed on the energy as if the air had turned to sugar.

But while that affects anyone who plays the game, it doesn't seem to bother me one way or another. I don't see them and I almost don't even hear them. I'm focused and when I do that I screen out a lot of things around me.

The guy I was guarding looked nervous and because I knew by then that he couldn't move left, I overplayed him to the right and when he turned to try to go left, I slipped a hand in, popped the ball away and started down court, fast, all alone, and I went in and rolled a pretty ordinary layup off the board and into the basket. Usually I'd have slammed it home. But the point was to make it look really easy, like I could do it anytime I wanted, like they were so bad I could make a play like that in my sleep. Head games. It worked.

They had no answer and they knew they had no answer and they gave up. Their coach called a time out and he worked them over pretty thoroughly, but he knew it wasn't gonna work. You could see the fear in their eyes.

I never show that. I can be getting hammered but it just doesn't show. All I do is focus harder and things come back to me. Fear is like a case of brain worms, the more you let it get to you the faster the worms work and pretty soon all you can do is go through the motions and when that happens you get your butt handed to you.

You'll hear guys talking about the zone and I think that a good part of that comes from being able to focus. You always hear how golf is a head game but, in fact, all sports are head games. It is always one-on-one. It's you against yourself, testing, pushing the limits, always taking your game to the next level ... if you can.

I coasted the rest of the way and Coach gave me plenty of rest and we won by thirty-two points. I also scored twenty-five points, the most I'd ever gotten, go figure. I mean, there I was favoring an ankle and they had to have known that and they still wouldn't come out on me and I just rained threes down on 'em. I also had twelve assists. Big night. Very big night. Joe slammed home thirty-one points.

And it wasn't over. I was scheduled to play my first prelim in the pool tournament at Shorty's at nine-thirty and Dad came with me. It was night time, after all, and even though the tournaments draw a different crowd, Dad was pretty uneasy about the night crowd at Shorty's. But then he'd played in a lot of pool halls in a lot of bad neighborhoods and I was not about to question his judgment.

To my surprise, Soc turned up too and even more surprising, he brought April and Marty and Lottie with him.

Talk about the winds of change, man. It was beginning to look like Socrates Keefer was running up a new set of sails. Or maybe not. He was still wearing his leathers and that jacket with the big snake on the back.

I introduced Dad to the girls and then we stood around talking while we waited for Shorty to call the players.

"You were absolutely awesome tonight," April said.

"Oh my God," Lottie said. "That steal at mid-court just wiped them out."

I could feel Soc watching me, waiting for my head to get up to something resembling a large hubbard squash, but I just grinned and nodded. "We played well," I said. "Guys got open, they knew where to be and they never stopped moving."

"And you got 'em the ball," April said.

I shrugged and out of the corner of my eye I saw Soc grin. "And now he's got to get it together and shoot some serious pool."

"Focus," I said.

"Concentration," he said.

"It's everything," Dad said.

I wound up at the front table shooting against a guy named Paul Wing. I didn't know anything about him, except that he came from out of town.

Maybe I didn't make it clear before, but this tournament was sanctioned and the top prize was twenty-five thousand bucks. The last two matches were going to be on television. I would even get to keep any money I won because winning a pool tournament doesn't make you a professional athlete in the eyes of the NCAA. Otherwise, I'd have had to play as an amateur.

Of course, I really was an amateur, but if I finished in the top ten I'd be considered a top player and the next time I played I'd actually be seeded. This was like an open tournament in golf, except that all the qualifying was done in the tournament.

You also had to pay to play. A hundred bucks. That's where some of the prize money came from. The rest was provided by the sponsor, which was Dad's company.

My opponent got to break and he knew what he was doing. He sank two balls on the break and then nailed the one and the two before leaving himself short in setting up his next shot. He played it safe and tried to bury the cue ball so I wouldn't have a shot and he did a good job of it.

Except that my signature at the pool table is using the cushions. I don't know why but I see the angles clearly, and

I lined up and stroked a shot that used three cushions and then kissed the five ball into the side pocket. Then I ran the table. The truth is, I'm better at pool than I am at basketball or even baseball, which I had always thought was my first sport. I told you, jocks run in the family.

I played four matches that night and only once did I face a challenge and that was when I left a shot on the table. My fault. I didn't draw the cue ball back far enough and I had to play it safe and I screwed that up too.

But the guy was overeager and after sinking three shots he tried a really thin cut shot, a shot that even good players miss as often as they make and he missed it and then I closed him out.

There were a lot of people shooting pool Friday night and they had been shooting since six o'clock. Shorty had scheduled me late because of the game.

By eleven-thirty I was through and I had moved way, way up in the standings. Even so, Saturday was gonna be a long day because they had to pare the field down to twelve players to play the twelve seeded players on Sunday. The final four players would be on television Sunday night.

Those people would most likely be the pros and they didn't play until Sunday because of their national rankings. All I had to do was go undefeated through about a dozen more matches and I'd get to play on Sunday and I wanted to know what it felt like to shoot against a pro.

Even though it was late I went off with Soc and the girls for pizza and Dad went home. He's cool. He knew.

We went to Nicolo's and got a table near the back and ordered up some serious pizza and soda and at first we talked and laughed and I began to think I'd done something wrong. They all seemed to be tiptoeing around me and I felt like an outsider again. I said very little and relaxed and tried to let the game come to me, but I could feel them watching me, especially April and Soc. I had the feeling that they were waiting for me to explode.

I wrote it off to their not knowing me very well and to the novelty of having Soc with them in a public place, an event, by the way, which caused considerable stir among the kids who were there, and as Nicolo's is always packed on a Friday night, it meant the rumors on Monday would be headline sort of stuff. It was gonna be jabber and chatter land.

Still, I had a good time. I was out with four people I liked and whatever else was going on, I was pretty sure they liked me. A new guy can't always be choosy about who he hangs with, but even if I had selected this group, I couldn't have made better choices.

Not until Soc and I were riding back to my house after dropping April off, did it hit me that someone had made those choices. Soc. He'd brought the girls, after all. He is a mysterious guy. He knows things. He sees things. He misses nothing.

"Pretty good night," he said.

Clearly an ambiguous remark. He could have been talking about me or he could have been talking about himself.

"Best ever," I said.

"You tore up the pea patch, man."

"I was talking about Nicolo's."

"You do make good choices."

"So do you. How'd you happen to pick those people?"

He grinned. "Saw you at lunch yesterday, remember? Then there was a rumor that you're taking April to the prom."

"Not a rumor. Fact."

"She's the best," Soc said.

"She said you've known each other since first grade."

"Never fooled her for a second. Everybody else bought into my bad-ass routines, but not April."

"What was going on at Nicolo's? I felt a little like a fifth wheel."

"What would you expect, man? You put on a show like that on the basketball court and then you blow every opponent away shooting pool? Those girls are all athletes. They know what that meant. They know that you almost never get to see a thing like that, let alone know the dude who pulled it off."

I laughed. "I never thought of that. I was too wrapped up in the games."

"But you got back to earth real quick. You never once

talked about it at Nicolo's. You just took a back seat and listened to us talking over old times. That was pretty cool."

"Okay, let's get off this before I lose track of who I am. I got a question. You just blew your cover. I mean, you totally shattered the image you've spent all this time building up. What's with that?"

"Probably get an A in gym too."

"This is getting serious. You gonna need counseling?"

"Sometimes things come to an end, that's all."

"We got about a half year left of high school," I said.

"And most of the applications are in and all we have to do is wait and find out where we'll be next year."

"Where did you apply?" I asked. "And how come we never talked much about this?"

"It didn't come up."

"But it has now."

"We got something else more important to talk about."

"The murders."

"Everybody seems to have forgotten. Nicolo's was back to normal. If I were a killer it'd be time to strike."

"We never finished with your list."

"What time will you be through tomorrow?"

"I play early. Nine. I'll be done by supper."

"I'll be over at seven. That okay?"

"You think he'll strike soon."

"Very soon. The tournament has brought him a whole

lot of victims and he seems to like people from out of town best."

"Which is why we need to do some homework."

"I can handle that."

He grinned. "But can you handle April?"

"It's a dead heat," I said.

"I think you're right. Be interesting to watch."

"You taking Lottie to the prom?"

"Whoa, picked that off, didn't you."

"Focus," I said.

"Concentration," he said.

"It's everything," I said.

17 Saturday

That night the weather turned warm and a soft rain began falling and as the warm air and rain eroded the snow it produced a heavy gray fog that buried the morning.

Nobody else was up and I made myself a poppy seed bagel with cream cheese and plenty of smoked salmon and chased it with a big glass of cold skim milk. There would be plenty of free coffee and doughnuts at Shorty's and he was also providing lunch for the players. He ran a classy tournament.

Because of the fog I left early and man it was really thick. I kept the car at a crawl, and I think that only because I knew the way so well from having driven it so often, did I get there. I'd never driven through so dense a fog and it was strange to realize that most of the time, until I passed something I recognized, I didn't know where I was.

Even then I wasn't certain and it made me doubly uneasy not being able to use the passage of time to help judge my progress. I had to let the car ease slowly along so what usually took a few minutes now took forever. Never had I felt more alone.

And yet, I got to Shorty's by seven-thirty, only a few minutes later than what I had planned and that gave me plenty of time to warm up. I had the place to myself except for Frenchy Livernois, who had already been out and pulled his lobster traps and now sat at the counter, watching me work through my normal routine.

First I worked on long shots, not worrying about sinking them so much as making sure my stroke was smooth and straight and that I followed through properly. I spent half an hour and the whole time Frenchy never said a thing until I stopped and took down my cue and tucked it carefully into the hard case.

"You shoot good," he said.

"Thanks." I poured myself a cup of coffee from the big urn, which was there along with a supply of doughnuts for the players.

"You think you can win?"

"Wouldn't play if I didn't," I said.

He laughed. "Well, you're cocky enough to win, I'll give you that," he said.

Frenchy is tall and slender and though I had never talked to him before, I had heard him talking to the other men and he was always friendly and he liked to laugh. He also had a reputation as the best fisherman in the fleet, a fact which, or so I gathered from what I'd heard, pretty much stuck in the craw of Black Jack Jones, the skipper of the *Sea Wolf*.

"How bad was the fog out there this morning?" I asked.

"Thick like a good winter soup."

"How do you find your pots when it's like that?"

He shrugged. "It used to take a long time. Now, I have locators on each buoy. My son, who is only twelve, suggested that and then he set it up for me. Kids, these days ..." he shook his head and smiled. "I don't think he'll be a fisherman."

"How does the system work?"

"You want to see?"

I looked at the clock. I had plenty of time. "Sure."

We walked down through the fog to the docks and every boat was tied up.

"Everybody's back already?" I asked.

He shook his head. "Nobody but me went out."

We stepped from the pier onto the boat and he opened the cabin and we stepped inside and he turned on the lights. It looked like the nerve center on a destroyer.

"I like gadgets," he said, "and some of them work pretty well." He turned a key in the console and I heard the generator start up and then he flipped on a computer screen. It showed a series of circles from the center out and here and there it showed groupings of numbered white dots.

He pointed to the dots. "Those are my traps," he said. "As I go toward them, the screen shows how close I am. You want, I'll take you out sometime."

Sounded like fun to me. "Sure," I said. "I'd like to see how it works." I looked back at the screen. "What kind of a thing do you put on the trap?"

He opened a drawer and picked up a small round object encased in plastic. It was about the size of a quarter and not much thicker.

"How does it stick to the trap?"

"It has a peel off on the back. The adhesive is water resistent and very strong. I tried to pull one off and I tore out a strip of wood from the trap."

"Could you track someone with it? I mean how far away can you pick up the signal?"

"Several miles on the water. I never tried it on land." He grinned. "Why, you need to keep track of someone?"

"I might." I looked at the signal device. "Do different ones give off different signals?"

"They do. I've got 'em marked on my chart. I could navigate just by following the signals, and this morning, in the fog, it was easier than checking my GPS." He grinned. "Who've you got in mind here?"

I didn't know what to say. "Suppose I was able to stick these to a couple of guys. If I alerted you, could you monitor where they were?"

"Why would I do that?"

"One of them might be the killer," I said.

He laughed. "What if he's not?"

I shrugged. "Then we try someone else."

"These puppies cost me over a hundred apiece," he said, "and I'm betting I wouldn't get them back."

"What if I paid you for them?"

"Wouldn't this be against the law?"

"What isn't?" I said.

He shook his head. "Not much, these days."

"I gotta talk to someone," I said. "Would you think about it? I mean, it might work."

"If you stick them to the right guy, which means you have someone you suspect."

"Two, maybe three."

"The killings have been pretty wildly scattered and, like I said, I can't promise anything on land."

"But it might be worth trying. Could it be hooked up to work with a portable, a lap top?"

"Let me think about it."

"It's a cool system," I said.

He shut off the screen and killed the generator. "Fishermen these days, gotta be high-tech. Most of the time I work alone because I can't find a deck hand." He swept his hand toward the gear. "Without this, I don't get out at all."

We walked outside and he locked the cabin door and we climbed up onto the pier. The fog had gotten thicker, a dense gray mass that shrouded the buildings and draped the cars parked along the street so you couldn't see them until you were a few feet away and I was beginning to think that maybe a lot of the players wouldn't be able to find Shorty's. Heck, I was a block away and I wasn't sure I could find it.

"I can't see a thing," I said.

"Just stay close. I'm used to the fog," Frenchy said. But used to the fog or not, the way he navigated was by keeping his right hand extended and brushing it along the cars.

He never once looked into any of the cars. But I did. I couldnt help it. When we got to the last car before we turned the corner I almost wished I hadn't.

He was sitting behind the driver's seat, his head back with a huge knife rammed through his chest.

I sang out and Frenchy turned and I was standing there with my mouth open, pointing toward the passenger side window.

He bent down and looked in. "Well, now, ain't that something," he said.

I reached into my pocket, took out my cell phone and punched in 911. Four out of five. How was it even possible? It couldn't be. But it was and for the first time I felt a little queasy.

Frenchy reached in through the open window and

touched the edge of the knife blade just below the hilt. "Somebody put a heck of an edge on that knife. It's even good steel."

That changed something. Before it had been just a knife, kind of a weird knife but a knife you could probably buy most anywhere. Maybe that was still true, but if Frenchy was right about the steel, then maybe the knife was expensive and that made a difference. Knowing that the killer had sharpened it, that he had worked at getting it ready to kill someone, also made a difference. It meant that he spent time preparing to kill.

While we waited for the cops I took a good long look. The knife was the same, the man had been stabbed in exactly the same place, right down through his necktie, and he was short, about five-five at most.

Lt. Colello accompanied us back to Shorty's where we sat at a table in the back and answered questions. There was nothing to say, really. All I'd done was happen to look into the car. But I could see that coincidence, as an explanation, was wearing thin. It was a matter of too many, too close together.

The clock read nine-ten and the other players were there and ready to go.

Shorty came over to the table. "Nick, Harley here's got a match to play. That gonna be okay?"

Lt. Colello grinned and looked around at me. "You ready to play?"

I shrugged. "Can't forfeit," I said.

"Then go to it. I'm through here for now. Just don't say anything about this until I go public. In fact, keep it absolutely quiet."

He saw the question in my eyes. "Harley, Frenchy, Shorty. Not a word. He may come back and I want to be waiting for him when he does."

We all agreed, and Shorty breathed a sigh of relief. A murder almost next door was not gonna help the reputation of the neighborhood and it would certainly affect any chance he had to host future tourneys. It might even affect the gate at this tournament because people had to park so far from the pool hall, and at five bucks a head, he couldn't afford to lose customers.

I opened my cue case, jointed my stick and put some powder on my bridge hand. Shoot pool. I was about to shoot pool. I kept saying it over and over, but I was having a lot of trouble getting the victim out of my mind.

My opponent, a guy named Raker, that's all, just Raker, broke and ran the first rack. That made it worse. I had to sit and watch and what I needed to do was shoot and hope that having to focus would clear my mind.

He broke and ran the second rack and I watched him closely, trying to decide whether he was that good or just lucky and hot. The more I watched, the more I thought maybe it was all three and that can be an impossible combination.

And then, halfway through the third rack, his concentration flickered and he left the cue ball buried and had to play a safe shot.

My shot, and from where he left the ball I knew he hadn't seen me play because he left me a two-cushion shot and a possible combination to sink the nine ball and take the game.

But it was a nasty shot. What I had to do was make sure I sunk the five and then put enough high right English on the cue to make it spin off the cushion and into the nine and nudge it into the corner pocket.

Very risky shot, because putting English on the cue ball might well cause me to miss the five and have to give the table back unless I sunk the nine.

No hesitation. You see it, you go for it. I told you before I see things on the pool table the same way I see things on the basketball court. I see them and then I know how to make them happen and I lined up on the cue and shot. The five ball went home into the side pocket and the cue came off the cushion just as I'd planned, headed toward the nine ball sitting just to the side of the corner pocket and then hit the cushion and cut the nine ball into the pocket.

From then on I was in the groove. I ran him out in straight games and by then other guys had showed up and all the tables were occupied.

I have no idea how they found their way through that fog, but they did. Shorty might just as well have had one of

Frenchy's beacons on the roof. In a way, he did. Money and fame. Things like that can overcome almost anything.

I don't think I ever had a longer day. After the first match, the guys I played had already won at least five matches and the competition had gotten hot. They could all shoot and luck as a factor in winning had suddenly assumed a larger role in the matches where skill levels ran close.

By the third match I was playing a guy who had already won eight matches (counting Friday night) just as I had. At that point you fight constantly to keep from making mistakes. The only time you play defense is when you don't have a shot. Otherwise it's all offense. The trick is to stay at your level of play and not start thinking you can make any shot on the table. One by one you clear the plate and go to the next break. Nothing fancy, nothing desperate because those are the shots that nine times out of ten, when you're under pressure, you miss.

I reduced my thinking as I played, forcing everything out of my mind but the cue and the ball I needed to sink. And Shorty and his wife Mary Anne did a masterful job of keeping track of the players and the tables, setting up the following matches and making sure no one played on the same table twice in a row. It was a big job, but as the day slid past there were fewer and fewer players.

My last match of the day started at four. You might not believe it because it was, after all, pool, but being in condition from basketball gave me an advantage. My legs stayed strong and full of spring and I just kept on shooting.

My last opponent of the day was a big guy, fat with great chubby fingers. I hadn't seen him play because I'd been playing, but he'd reached the same level I had so I knew he'd be good.

He won the break but when he lined up and slammed the cue ball into the nine-ball rack, I knew he was tired. I saw it in the way he left his follow-through short. As a result the balls that should have gone down on the break were still on the table and it was my shot.

I felt like I was moving in to spear a wounded lion. One by one the balls disappeared and finally the eight went down and it left me a tap in on the nine. My break. I dropped two balls and I ran the table and never looked back.

Dad was there as he had been since my second match, sitting quietly, watching. I never once looked his way. He'd taught me that. Never take your eyes off the table.

Not until I sank that final ball did I truly look up. I'd gotten into Sunday. I'd reached my first goal. Now I had another. Shoot in the finals.

As I took down my cue and stored it in its case I saw a number of men go up to Dad, shake hands and talk and then move on. They were the seeded players, the pros on the tour, the older guys, and they all seemed to know Dad.

The thing is, I knew he had played in a lot of tournaments, but it had suddenly become clear that he was something of a legend among the people who played the game. How is it, I wonder, that we always seem to know so little about our parents as we grow up?

It wasn't a question I could answer, or one that I was sure I could ever answer, but just then it was enough to know something about him that I hadn't known before.

And anyway, a much bigger question needed an answer and I was already looking forward to meeting with Soc. The murders simply had to stop.

18 Soc Surprises

Dad insisted I leave my car and ride home with him because the fog had gotten worse.

"You had a heck of a day," he said.

"I think I got pretty lucky on some of those shots."

"Nope. There's no luck on the pool table. You make shots or you don't."

"Nobody makes all their shots," I said.

"The difference is that good players find a way to make up for their mistakes. You did that today. Last night you were just hot. Today you played pool."

"Now there's tomorrow," I said.

"Worried?"

"They're all pros, Dad."

"Sure, but not every pro has a good day every time out."

"Me either," I said.

"It makes the game worth playing."

"It's a great game."

"The best."

I looked at him carefully, not sure whether I should ask. Then I did. "Why did you quit?"

He smiled. "I wasn't going to make a living playing pool unless I turned to gambling and I wouldn't do that. The tournaments were small and there was almost never a big enough pot and even when the pot was big the money didn't go far enough down the list."

"You could still do it," I said.

"I could. But I've finally reached the point where I don't have to travel much and the thing is, Harley, I like my job and I like the company. Mostly, I just like being home more. Maybe when Janey goes off to college I could do it again as long as Mom wanted to travel with me."

"Might be fun."

"It might. But I've had about all of living on the road that I want."

"You were really good, weren't you? I mean, all those guys, all those pros who kept coming over to say hello. They all know who you are, don't they?"

"The old guys, anyway."

"How many tournaments did you win?"

"Oh, I don't know. Quite a few. My winnings bought our first house. Gave us a good start."

"Don't you miss it?"

"Sometimes. Not often."

I shook my head. "It's such a rush," I said.

He laughed. "It is that. But the other side is the times you lose, the times you should win and you don't. And there's nobody to talk to. Not one of those guys you saw talking to me today has been to college or even read a book. Maybe some of the younger players have, but not many."

"I want to win," I said.

"You're good enough, you know. Or maybe you don't know. I do. I know those guys. I know how well they play. You can take them."

"As long as my head doesn't get in the way."

"Of course."

We rode along in the fog and suddenly I was thinking about the guy in the car, the latest one. Sure, I wasn't supposed to tell anyone, but I didn't think that meant my parents. "There was another murder this morning."

"What?"

"And I saw him."

"Again? I don't believe this!"

"I went for a walk to see Frenchy Livernois's boat and on the way back I saw him. It was just the same." I told him the rest of the story. "Lt. Colello told us not to say anything until he does. Something about keeping the guy on edge."

Dad nodded. "So he'll make a mistake."

"Yeah, something like that."

"And with that on your mind, you still qualified."

"I think I'm a little weird, Dad. But the same thing happens on the basketball court. All I see is the game."

"I wondered about that. The crowd never seems to affect you, does it?"

"Most of the time I don't even hear 'em."

"Part of the reason I quit," he said, "was because more and more I was aware of the spectators. I've often wondered if that happened because I was ready to move on."

"I'm not following," I said.

"Sometimes, I think, we make unconscious decisions about things and then we begin to change direction a little at a time. But it takes awhile to see it."

"Okay, this is pretty much going past me."

He laughed. "But at least now you know it can happen and maybe when it does you'll see it sooner. That will be useful, I think."

Soc was waiting for me when I got home, sitting in the kitchen with a big piece of apple pie and a cup of coffee and talking to Mom and Janey.

He was a different guy again. His ponytail was gone and his hair had been cut short. He was wearing jeans and a collared shirt and a pullover sweater and running shoes and he looked like a normal sort of guy. In fact, he looked kind of preppy and that was way too improbable.

Even more improbable was the fact that he had them both

laughing and relaxed and obviously taken with his charm. Charm? Socrates Keefer? Charming?

Janey looked up. "Why didn't you tell me?" she asked.

"What? What didn't I tell you?"

"That you asked April to the prom! My God, Harley, how can you not tell us something like that?"

I shrugged and cut a piece of pie, trying to figure out how I was gonna get around this conversation. It was making me feel kind of squirrely.

Dad helped. "What you ought to know is that Harley is in the Sunday matches. He cleaned house."

I accepted everyone's congratulations but if I thought it was gonna change Janey's focus I was mistaken.

"Are you gonna wear a tux?" she asked.

"I don't know." I turned to Soc. "Is it formal?"

"Yeah. You gotta wear a tux."

"So I rent a tux."

"What kind of corsage will you get April?" Janey asked.

I poured a glass of milk and sat. "I don't know. I haven't even thought about it."

"You have to decide these things, Harley. First you have to know what color gown April will be wearing and then get a corsage to match the gown."

"How do you know this stuff?" I asked.

"All girls know these things, Harley. They're important!"

"Okay, we'll talk it over and you can help me get it right."

"She's going to wear white," Janey said. "An evening dress, not a gown, straight and long with long white gloves and white satin shoes. The jewelry is still up in the air."

Stunned? Of course. I'd only asked her yesterday. Which meant, as far as I could see, that the only thing she'd been missing was a date. I guessed maybe I'd been living on a boy's planet, but to tell you the truth, I had no plans to leave.

I was even a little insulted, but the thing about having a sister is that I knew that what had gone on before had nothing to do with me, and now had everything to do with me. Girls prepare well ahead for things like proms.

I didn't mention the murder until Soc and I had repaired to my quarters over the garage. He listened carefully and then shook his head and pulled several folded sheets of notebook paper from his back pocket.

"I've been going over and over this and I think it's the same guy that did the killings in Black Springs. What I did was ask my Dad if he could remember anyone moving into town about the time of those killings."

"He could remember that?"

"It was a lot smaller town then. It's only grown since the turnpike went in seven years ago. Before that it was only a big town during the summer. In the winter it was pretty much deserted." He unfolded the papers. "He came up with three names and they're all still here. Two of them were on my original list. Cuccinello at the comic store, Roadkill Renkler,

The captain of the *Sea Wolf*, Black Jack Jones, wasn't. Cuccinello and Jones moved here about that time but Roadkill grew up here and went west and then, after his father ran off, he came back to take care of his mother."

"Whoa, now this is getting interesting. You think we should call Lt. Colello?"

"I already did."

"And…"

He shook his head. "I don't think he was interested. He said they weren't on his list of suspects."

"Why not? Did he say?"

"He just told me to leave it to him."

"But that's what he would have to say, isn't it?"

"Sure."

"Okay, where do we go from here?" I asked.

"We look for connections, then we check 'em out. Roadkill is a wide body guy with gray hair. Not fat, just really big. He's about five ten or so."

I shivered. "That's pretty close to the description I gave Lt. Colello."

"Black Jack also fits that description. Cuccinello's a little overweight, and like I told you, he's taller than you, but in the dark it might be hard to tell the difference."

"I've seen Renkler and Black Jack at Shorty's. That's where I first saw Black Jack. He comes in there, buys a beer in the bar and then comes into the pool room. So does Renkler.

Neither of them talks to anyone."

"Cuccinello's store is three doors up and he eats his lunch in the bar."

"Whoa, this is hot," I said. "We can connect all three of them to Shorty's. I think we're onto something here."

And suddenly I knew what had been hanging in the back of my mind. "Maybe the killer picks out his victims at Shorty's?"

"It seems likely."

"Were any of them there last night?"

"Yup. All three," Soc said.

"So now what?"

"We check 'em out."

"Just like that? Soc, I don't know anything about stuff like this. How do you check people out?"

"First you check where they live."

"Like what? Break in?"

"If you have to."

"No. No way." I'd had one run-in with Black Jack. And frankly, any guy who lived on road kills was high on my list of people who could hit a perfect ten on my weird-o-meter. And then I remembered Frenchy.

"Here's something," I said, and then I told him about the system that Frenchy used to find his lobster pots."

Soc grinned. "All we gotta do is find a way to stick the thing to them where they won't be found."

"Got any ideas?"

"I'll think of something. Maybe during the tournament when it's really crowded. I could get close enough then. But we still have to search their houses."

"Soc, we're talking a killer here, right? And don't I seem to remember my mother being real clear on staying from anyone like that? Yes, I do!"

He ignored me. "We'd have to know where they were. One of us could stand watch and the other do the search and we could keep a cell line open if things got too close."

"Is this getting a little too crazy? Because I think maybe we're getting off the map here."

"Com'on," Soc said. "Let's go for a ride."

We went for a ride. What was I gonna do, not go?

19   Getting Answers

But there was no getting out of the house without eating supper and Mom invited Soc to stay and he, of course, called home to clear it with his Mom, simply because that's the way you do things.

An hour later we were headed back to Shorty's and we hit it lucky. All three of our suspects were there watching the tournament.

We stayed for about a half hour and then drifted away and headed first up to Cowper Lane where Black Jack Jones lived in a little Cape-style house, set back from the road.

"How are we gonna get in?" I asked.

"We'll find a way. I'm gonna park the car at the back of the public parking lot. You'll keep watch and we'll keep the cell phones connected."

"Okay."

So there I sat, not in the truck, but down near the corner in a patch of bushes, waiting and watching, and looking at my watch over and over, and checking around me for the least sound of someone sneaking up behind.

It took Soc about twenty minutes and despite the raw cold, I was sweating hard.

We didn't talk until we were inside the car. "What'd you find?"

"Nothing. There just isn't much in the house. I think he spends most of his time on the boat and probably only sleeps in the house when it gets too cold. He doesn't even have a TV. And there's no phone. I went through every drawer, every closet but it all looked perfectly normal."

"What now? Cuccinello?"

"Shorty's to make sure they're still there. Then we'll try Roadkill's. We may not get to Cuccinello tonight. But more and more I'm thinking we need to focus on Roadkill."

"Why?"

"I asked my Uncle Henry about him and he said that Roadkill's father was the meanest man he ever met. He beat his son and his wife all the time. And get this ... he was a traveling salesman and he ..."

"What?"

"Yeah." He grinned. "Amazing, huh? But there's more. When Roadkill's father was out of town, and he was gone for weeks at a time, his mother rented rooms to traveling salesmen."

"Uh-oh."

"It's almost too good."

He started the car and we headed to Shorty's.

"What do you know about psychology?"

"Nothing."

"I've been reading up on it. If I remember, you said all the victims have been short, right?"

"Five-four to five-five."

"So was Roadkill's father. What that could mean is that each time Roadkill kills, he's killing a short traveling sales-man, or ... in his mind he's killing his father. It's kind of like he's getting even."

"Psychology tells you that?"

"Well, not exactly, but it talks a lot about symbolic be-havior."

"You're losing me here."

"In this case the victims are symbols of his real father, kind of like pinch hitters."

"What an awesome concept."

"I thought it was pretty cool."

"But how much do you trust your uncle's stories?"

"Uncle Henry and Aunt Claire are the nosiest people in town. But a lot of their stories check out."

"So maybe this story is true, and if it is ..."

"Then maybe we know what sets him off."

"You want me to talk to Frenchy about a locator?"

"See if you can get him to give you one and I'll slip into

the crowd and stand next to Roadkill."

"He can't suspect."

Soc grinned. "He won't."

Back at Shorty's Soc watched one of the games in progress while I worked through the crowd until I reached Frenchy. It was a good spot.

Roadkill stood near the back of the room where he always stood, and we were hidden from him in the little alcove by the end of the service counter.

"How's it going?" I asked.

Frenchy turned. "I haven't seen anyone you can't beat."

"That's the kind of news I like to hear."

"You checking the competition?"

"Sort of. I wondered about those signaling devices."

Frenchy grinned. "I thought you might be." He reached into his pocket, pulled out a manila envelope folded in half, and handed it to me down low, where no one could see.

"Inside, I wrote down my cell phone number. The software's in there. All you have to do is download it. Then follow the instructions. It's pretty simple." He reached into his other coat pocket and took out a small black box with two wires coming from it, and handed it to me. "Plug this into your computer and hang the wire out a window. This is the receiver for the signal. The whole town is displayed but you'll have to zoom in and out to know exactly where he is. If you have any trouble, give me a call."

I put the stuff in my jacket pockets. "Thanks. This is really gonna help."

"How soon is this gonna happen?"

"Pretty soon. We'll get the sensor on him tonight."

"Sooner the better. Before he kills someone else."

"Have you tried this out on land?"

He grinned. "I had my wife driving all over town. There's only one spot I couldn't track and that's over in the northwest corner. The hills over there blocked the reception."

"That'll do just fine."

"Still can't tell me who it is, huh?"

"We have to be sure. I mean, what if we've picked some innocent guy?"

"You'd be in a peck of trouble."

"Yeah. Not good."

I spotted Soc, and using my eyes to signal, I glanced back at the rest rooms and we both headed in that direction.

"Thanks again for the help," I said.

"Glad to do it. And don't forget, when the waters warm, we've got a date for some bluefishing."

"I won't." I said.

Inside the men's room I handed him the signalling device. "The back peels off," I said. "It'll stick to anything and it'll stay there."

"Okay. When we go back out, turn toward Roadkill and I'll be behind you. When you're close, I'll push you into him as if I'd stumbled and just as you hit him, I'll stick this under his coat."

"Good thing we decided to piss first," I said.

"You nervous?"

"You're not?"

"Nope."

"Then you're not human."

"I just don't get nervous. I like pressure."

At the end of the hall I turned to the left and when I was inches from Roadkill, Soc shoved me from behind and I banged into Roadkill hard. "Hey, what the heck is this!" I grunted as I grabbed onto Roadkill's shoulder to keep from falling.

"Hey! Watch it!" he said.

"Sorry, somebody banged into me. You okay?"

"Sure. Sure." He shook his head. "Just watch it."

"Sorry," I said and then worked my way through the crowd and out the door where Soc was waiting.

It took twelve minutes to get to Roadkill's house and it took me by surprise. It was a nice old house, a large federal with weathered shingles and it was neat and the trim had been painted recently.

It certainly didn't fit a guy named Roadkill who worked on the town crew.

Soc hid the truck up a narrow dirt road about three hundred yards from the house and we walked back and I took up station where I could see the road and the driveway.

I wished I'd had time to set up the locator on my computer, but we had no time for that yet.

Still, I thought we'd be okay. The tournament would run another hour and it would take at least twelve minutes for Roadkill to get here, so we had time. What I didn't figure on was how long it would take Soc to search the house.

It was a big house with two floors and a wing off the back. I waited forty minutes and then I spoke into the phone.

"Soc? Can you hear me?"

"Yeah."

"We haven't got a whole lot longer."

"I've still got two rooms to go."

"If the tournament gets over sooner, he'll be here."

"Keep watching."

I watched. I waited. My legs were twitching and I was beginning to shake when I saw a pickup turn onto the road.

"Soc, there's a pickup coming slowly."

"Almost done."

And then the truck turned into the driveway and headed around to the back of the house.

"Soc! Now! Get out! He's around the back!"

The next thing I knew the front door opened and Soc legged it down the shoveled path to the road and then up to where I was waiting.

"That was way too close," I said.

He grinned. "Really gets the old heart pumping, doesn't it? Just like a close game."

"Let's get out of here, okay? I need something to eat."

"We got one more thing to check."

And then I remembered the dog. Roadkill had a nasty German shepherd. "How did you get past the dog?" I asked.

Soc pulled a plastic bag out of his pocket and held it up. "Venison. No dog can resist it. I'm not even sure I needed it. All he did was wag his tail and rub against my leg so I'd pet him. Shows you what rumors are worth."

The parking lot at Shorty's was still full and we had to park way down by the waterfront, which left us walking back up to Shorty's, along streets that didn't have anywhere near enough streetlights to suit me. But at least there were two of us and one of us could handle himself. All I could do was run. And while I wasn't all that fast, I figured it was gonna be an old white guy chasing me and no way could someone like that catch me.

As I climbed out of Soc's truck I looked down along the pier at the boats and stopped. The lights were on in the *Sea Wolf*. Black Jack Jones was at home.

"Hey, Soc ..." I pointed toward the big boat.

"Yeah," he said. "I saw it. He must be getting ready for an early start in the morning. Probably sleep on board."

How did he know that? Well, how could he not know it? Working for his father he was out and around town all the time. If anybody knew what was going on, it'd be someone like Soc. Nothing seemed to get past him. He saw stuff that I walked right by. He heard things I never did.

He locked the car and we started walking toward Shorty's. Two of the lights on the street along the pier were out. Not good. At any second I expected some maniac to come rushing out of the dark with a huge knife.

My heart was running at aerobic speed and I could feel the sweat running icy cold down my sides.

Then Soc said … "is this fun or what? Man, he could be waiting for us in any one of those alleys up ahead."

Fun? No, it was not fun. It was an exercise in pure terror! "Are you nuts?"

"Sure. Absolutely. I love stuff like this. Makes me feel really energized."

"Makes me want to fill my pants."

He chuckled. "But you won't, you know."

"I don't know that at all!" I said. He was beginning to piss me off.

"Sure you do. Guys like you don't come apart when there's trouble. If you did, you couldn't play basketball the way you do."

"Soc, in case you didn't notice, nobody on the basketball court is carrying a knife."

He laughed. "They might as well be," he said.

"I gotta tell you, this is going over my head." All the time

I kept my eyes glued to the dark places. "Besides he's at his house."

"Maybe."

"Why would he come back here?"

"Maybe he didn't have one of those knives with him and he spotted another victim."

"That makes me feel a whole lot better."

We kept to the side of the street by the pier, which was six feet below street level. Only where the steps went down was there any danger because someone coming over a six-foot high wall was not gonna be moving real quick, and if he came at us from the far side of the street, we'd have plenty of warning. Even if we didn't see him right off we'd hear him because despite all the cars parked along the street there was hardly a sound: no wind from the water, nothing.

And then I heard the sound of someone running ... fast and coming closer and I stopped. We hunkered down until our profiles disappeared and we slipped into the dark.

Closer and closer the runner came and then suddenly a guy burst into the light. A jogger. That's all. Just a jogger.

We stood back up.

"What a rush!" Soc said. "Man, was that cool or what? I thought my heart was gonna leap right out of my chest!"

"Whatta you say we jog the rest of the way," I said.

"No, man, we gotta walk. Maybe it'll draw him out."

"I'm pretty sure I wouldn't like that," I said.

"We can take him," Soc said.

"What makes you so sure? You're talking crazy here, like lunatic! Guys like that don't go down easy!" Okay, it was a guess. I'd never dealt with anyone who was nuts but I had this idea that anyone crazy enough to run around stabbing people was probably not rational and I remembered reading that people like that don't respond to pain the way normal people do.

Soc stopped and held up his hand, listening, looking around.

"What is this?" I whispered. "Are you trying to scare me?"

He held his finger to his lips and pointed to an alley across the street and then dropped into a crouch and crossed the street, using the parked cars for cover. I did the same. What choice did I have? Stay there alone? Not likely.

I hunkered down behind the car and then I saw Soc move and something glinted in the light and I looked at a long, dagger-like knife that he'd drawn from beneath his coat. In his left hand he held a small flashlight. He waited, listening, his eyes focused on the dark of the alley.

And then suddenly he stood up and turned on the light. The powerful beam lit up the alley and I saw a big shape rise up and dash back down the alley into the dark.

"That's him!" Soc said. "Com'on, we can run him down!"

I grabbed his arm and stopped him. "No! No way! He's

got too many places to hide."

He relaxed. "You're right," he said. "It's too much in his favor. Did you get a look at him?"

"Just a shape."

"Yeah, that's all I saw. But we know this. He's a big guy."

"So are all three of our suspects. You think we should call your godfather?"

"Naw. We don't even know for sure it was him. Could have been some derelict."

"We have derelicts in Yellow Springs?"

"In this neighborhood we do."

"No way."

We walked in the middle of the street, turning at the corner and now the lights were bright all the way to Shorty's and we just walked along, saying nothing.

Inside Shorty's there were people at the back ten tables and as usual the front four tables were empty. The tournament had finished for the night and Soc wandered around while I checked the pairings for Sunday. It was gonna be a long day.

Soc spotted Black Jack in the bar and Cuccinello was there too. Neither one looked as if he had been running. But could Roadkill have gotten back here that quickly? Why would he have done that? Had he seen Soc at the house? Or had Soc left something out of place?

Too many questions.

We drove to Nicolo's, ordered up a large pizza and a pitcher of Coke and settled into a booth near the back.

"I never asked what you found at Roadkill's."

"Interesting. In a drawer in a rolltop desk I found a series of clippings from the Black Springs newspaper. They were old and yellowed and the dates on them means they were clipped when the murders there occurred."

"Whoa."

"But all it means is that he was there."

"Circumstantial."

"Absolutely."

"Nothing else."

"Not enough time. It's a big house. He could have stuff hidden anywhere." He took a long swallow of Coke. "One thing I found is that the guy really knows how to sharpen a knife. Every one of the knives in the kitchen had an edge you could shave with."

"It's him. It has to be him."

"Hey guys, mind if I join you?"

It was Cuccinello. I looked over at Soc. "Hey, Cooch, yeah grab a spot, man."

"It was a long night." Cooch slid into the booth. "I been starving for the last hour."

20 Suspect

Cooch is three inches taller than I am and he's about as wide as a 1950's Buick Roadmaster, and I thought a guy like that could eat a lot. I glanced at the last two pieces of our pizza.

He saw me and laughed. "I already ordered. By phone. It'll be here any second. A super large."

"I never heard of a super large," I said.

"Special order. Only for certain people." He laughed. "Nick and I are old, old friends. I eat here every night."

It had taken seconds for him to demolish my belief that he could be a suspect. Okay, I'm gullible. I'm also naive or maybe I never knew enough bad guys. Maybe I never knew *any* bad guys, but no matter. There was no way Cooch was a serial killer."

He looked around at me. "I hear you qualified," he said.

"I did. I'm not sure how, but I did."

"Can you beat your old man?"

"About half the time."

"I saw him play once. Man, he was awesome!"

I hadn't thought about how old Cuccinello was until then, but now I guessed he might be the same age as Dad. I tried to put a picture in my mind of the guy I had seen in the alley and Cooch didn't fit. He was too tall, way too tall. A few inches might not have made much difference, but he was about six-six and I wouldn't have missed that.

"He taught me how to play," I said.

Cooch grinned and I gotta tell you, his grin is infectious. He grins, you grin back. "Word around here is that you'll go way up."

"I'm planning on winning," I said.

"Good. Never settle for second."

Soc got into the conversation. "You got anything new in the knife case?"

"Yeah, but they're really pricey. I just got my annual allocation of Randalls." He shook his head. "Three different style Bowies." He shook his head. "Those things are over five hundred bucks. I got ten different styles right now. Man, they go fast. You interested?"

"Sure," Soc said. "You gonna be open tomorrow?"

"You wanna see 'em, we can go there after we eat."

"You'd open just for me?" Soc said.

"Sure, Soc. Heck, you're one of my best customers."

Now what was I supposed to make of that? Soc had a big

interest in knives. It brought back all the rumors, but of course that was nuts because I'd been with him when we found two of the bodies. But it shows you how your imagination can push you in the wrong direction sometimes. I wondered if I'd been too quick in dismissing Cuccinello as a suspect.

From then on mostly he talked to Soc. The conversation ran to knife makers all over the country and what they were producing. I won't say it wasn't interesting, but I was beginning to think about getting some sleep. After all, I had to play in the final round starting at nine a.m.

And then Cooch's pizza came. It took up nearly the whole table and I never saw so much meat; sausage and pepperoni and bacon and then a mountain of peppers and mushrooms and onions and I don't even know what else on one pizza. But no dead fish, no anchovies. Cooch was apparently a man of good taste.

An hour later we walked back up the street to the Comic Shop. Cooch only turned on the lights in the back of the store and inside the main knife case.

The big polished steel blades gleamed in the light.

"Whoa," Soc said, "they're the best yet."

And they were. I'd never seen anything like them. The biggest had a blade over a foot long.

"Out of my league," Soc said.

"We could make a deal. You pay me off when you can."

"How long before they're all gone?" Soc asked.

"A week, maybe two. Sometimes they're gone by the end of the first day. It depends on who comes in. Whenever I get Randalls in I call people who've asked about them."

I could see he was tempted and I knew he had money because of the plowing.

"You oughta get one, Soc," Cooch said. "If you don't you'll have to wait a long time. These Bowies are real hard to get. I ordered these three years ago."

Soc shook his head. "Let me think about it over night," he said.

"You'll be at the tournament in the morning?"

Soc grinned. "Wouldn't miss it."

"Which one do you want? I'll set it aside." Cooch said.

Soc pointed.

"Good choice. The Smithsonian Bowie. Classic."

"How many knives do you sell a year?" I asked.

"Thousands." He waved his hand toward the front of the store. "The comics are a sideline. Most of my money comes from selling knives. Top quality stuff."

"Anything like the knives used in the murders?" I asked.

"The only fantasy knives I carry are Hibbens. Nick brought the murder weapons for me to look at. They sell for about sixty bucks and they're made in Pakistan. Better than the usual junk, but not up to my standards, though the steel was pretty good and they'd been sharpened beautifully."

"Where would you buy a knife like that?" I asked.

"About a thousand places on the Internet."

"You had any thoughts about this guy?" Soc asked.

"I try not to think about things like that." He grinned and waved his hand toward the front of the store. "I got enough violent stuff in this place." He rubbed his chin. "I'll tell you this, though. Guys like him, serial killers, I mean, they're the hardest to catch."

"I read that," I said.

"Nick says they almost never get caught until they want to get caught. They reach a point where they can't stand what they're doing but they can't stop."

"Crossed wires," Soc said.

"More like shorted out," Cooch said. He looked around at Soc and then at me. "I hear you guys saw a couple of the bodies."

"Yeah," Soc said. "Pretty ugly stuff."

"I can't stand the sight of blood," Cooch said. "I faint." He chuckled. "Kind of weird, huh? A guy selling all those knives and he can't stand the sight of blood."

"What difference would it make, I mean, how often do you cut yourself with them?" I asked.

"Never. Mostly I don't even take them out of their boxes except to make sure the numbers match. Once I cut my hand and I passed out and I was just lucky I didn't hit a major artery or I'd have bled to death."

We laughed, but the thing is, even though he laughed

with us, there was a look in his eyes that I couldn't define; wild and glazed like he'd been smoking gonge and yet, not like that, exactly. But a second ago it hadn't been there.

Things were getting weird. I kept pouncing on ordinary information as if it were evidence, which meant I was way too far over the top on this whole thing.

We walked back past Shorty's and down along the pier toward where we'd parked. Up ahead I could see the truck sitting in the dark. The street light above it had been on when we parked, but now it was out. I noticed that but I didn't pay much attention, and that's hard to explain.

"Well," Soc said, "what did you think?"

"He doesn't seem like a killer, exactly."

"Or he wants us to think that."

"He wouldn't want us to think anything else, would he?"

"No."

"So?"

"I don't know what to think," Soc said. "I mean, that thing about the salesman seemed to sew it up for Carol, and yet...

"Carol?"

"That's Roadkill's real name."

"As if he didn't have enough to piss him off, he's got a girl's name?"

"The thing is," Soc said, "we need to nail him cold. I mean we have to have absolute rock-solid evidence."

"Would you rule out Cooch?"

"Yeah, I think I would. Heck, Nick even brought the knives down there for him to look at."

"Which would have been a good trick, wouldn't it?"

"Sure."

"You know what I'm thinking?" I said. "I'm thinking I need to get home and get some sleep. I got a long, long day tomorrow, and all this thinking about who killed cock robin is beginning to eat at me."

We stopped at the car and as I waited for Soc to open the door, I looked down the line of boats to the *Sea Wolf*. The lights were still on in the cabin but I couldn't see anyone moving around.

The latch in the door clicked and I opened the door and climbed into the car, closing the door behind me, relieved at getting out of sight and off the street.

I heard the movement in the back seat at the same instant I heard Soc holler.

"Get out!"

And we did. Hurling the doors open and half-falling and half-rolling out onto the street and then running until we reached the next light. I already had my cell phone out and Soc had pulled out his knife.

"Are you okay?" he asked.

"I guess so. My ankle hurts a little, but I think it's okay." I looked around at him, waiting for someone to answer the phone at the police station. And that's when I noticed the blood on his jacket.

"Hey, did he get you?" I asked.

"It's okay, I think."

But I could see he was looking woozy.

When they answered the phone I couldn't stop shouting. And in the meantime Soc had pulled off his jacket and his arm was covered with blood, bright red blood, the stuff that comes from arteries. Slowly, he settled onto the street.

He clamped his hand over the wound and applied as much pressure as he could, but he was weak and I moved his hand away, tore the sleeve from his shirt and wound it around his arm above the long cut. I made it into a sort of tourniquet and as I tightened down the blood began to slow and then finally stop.

In the distance I could hear the sirens and I loosened the tourniquet, let the blood flow, and then tightened it again, silently thanking my mother for having insisted I take that course in first aid.

And then the ambulance rounded the corner and pulled up and the EMT's jumped out and took over.

"Is he okay?" I asked.

"He'll be okay. We'll get him to the hospital." They loaded him onto the gurney and slid it into the ambulance and they were pulling out when Lt. Colello arrived.

I didn't think I was gonna get a whole lot of sleep.

21 Sunday On Sunday

Fourteen stitches is what it took to close the wound and it would have been a lot worse if Soc hadn't been wearing his leather coat. The thick leather, designed to protect you if your bike goes down and you end up skidding over the pavement, had slowed the knife just enough to keep the blade from slicing deeply into the muscle, except in one spot. And the angle of the knife meant the slice into the muscle was from top to bottom instead of across, which is much worse. But he had lost a lot of blood and they had to give him a transfusion.

I left the hospital after midnight and I didn't get to sleep till sometime around two, which left me about five hours sleep and a long day ahead. Not the best situation.

And yet, as it turned out, not the worst either. I don't even remember dreaming, and that, for me, is rare. One second I was awake and the next the alarm was going off.

I have a great alarm clock. It plays the theme music from

Wallace and Gromit and I always wake up smiling, which is the only way to wake up. Bells, buzzers, and radio music always leave me irritated.

That doesn't mean I wasn't groggy, but after a couple of cups of coffee my eyes began to open, and I staggered out the door to my car and drove down to Shorty's.

The temperature had dropped as the front came through and now it felt like winter again, cold and dry with the wind out of the northwest instead of coming in off the water.

As I warmed up and sipped at yet another cup of coffee I went over what had happened last night.

Remembering was not helping my game. Pool requires absolute precision and repeating those precise movements time after time requires focus … concentration. But my mind kept drifting back to the night before. I was missing something. I had seen something, or heard something, and I couldn't remember what it was. Or maybe it wasn't a matter so much of remembering as not being able to see clearly.

It's like what happens when I'm taking a test and I come to a question I can't answer right away? That's what it was like. The answer was there, floating free in my mind but I couldn't pin it down.

So what I did was shoot the same shots over and over, trying to narrow my focus and after about an hour my game began to come together.

By the time my first match came up I was mostly there

and I got lucky and drew the break. Not my best break, but I sank the three ball and left myself a clear shot at the one and then set up for the two and then I ran the table.

The trick in any sport is to never have to do anything flashy. You always need to leave yourself in a position to accomplish what needs to be done with the least amount of effort. Never waste energy. Never try to impress anyone. My opponent never got to the table.

That kind of pumped me up. Maybe too much. But I got lucky. I didn't get the break and I had to sit and watch my opponent run the first rack. It gave me a chance to watch.

Always you look for weaknesses. Everybody has them. I don't like shots when the cue ball is too close to the rail. This guy avoided shots that required more than one cushion.

Why is it, when we know we have a weakness, that we keep leaving ourselves in a position that exposes the weakness? At that level any player should be able to avoid that and yet I knew that he was two or three shots away from leaving himself with a two cushion shot.

It came on the third shot and he missed and I cleaned up the seven, eight, and nine and then I broke. I know my weakness and I knew where I had to leave the cue ball to make the next shot. I worked my way up the table, never having to take a shot longer than half the table.

I screwed up just once and let him back on the table but he was too eager and one rack later I was back on for good.

Between the second and third match I had to wait for another match to finish and I sat and looked around. Black Jack was there, Cooch was there, and so was Roadkill. And here was the problem: they all looked too tall. And yet I didn't doubt for a second that one of them was the killer. Go figure.

Cooch smiled when I looked at him and gave me a thumbs up, and I nodded back at him. Now, how could he be a killer? A nice guy like that.

I was still thinking about that when the next match started and it got in my way. But so did my opponent. John Ragg. He'd won some small tournaments and he was ranked in the top hundred players in the country.

For the first time I had to beat a ranked player and that meant total focus and I was a long way from that. I managed to sink two balls on the break and I ran the table and then in the second rack I blew a simple cut shot and he ran three racks before he left himself with an impossible shot and played a safe.

And he played it well, leaving me a very difficult three-cushion shot or having to play a safety. No guts no glory, right? And this is what you save your flashy shots for. I lined it up and stroked it the length of the table, catching the left cushion just below the three-quarter mark. The ball then caromed off the end cushion and back toward the eight ball lying close behind the nine near the side pocket.

It wasn't a matter of just coming off the cushions, it was

also a matter of getting the pace right so the cue ball would just nudge the eight into the side and then stop to leave me a shot on the nine into the cross side. I don't think I ever made a better shot.

We were tied at three games apiece and then I got back into my game and ran the table. I felt like I'd played four full quarters of fast-break, full-court press basketball and now I had to step up and do it again.

Between games I sat on the stool and Dad came over and draped his arm over my shoulders.

"How're you doing?"

"I'm okay," I said.

"That was one heck of a shot."

I shook my head. "I don't want to have to do that again."

"I stopped at the hospital on the way over and Soc says he'll be here later so you have to keep on winning."

I grinned. "It's getting tough, Dad."

"Fun, isn't it?"

Well, that was not what I'd been thinking. In fact, I had felt myself getting closer and closer to panic. But he was right. It was fun. This was what I had been shooting at for years. I shook my head and grinned at him. "Yeah," I said. "It's fun. But it's also scary."

"S'what makes it fun," he said. He looked over at the big board to see who I had to play next. "Okay. Pete Folsom. Good player. Past his prime. Still ranked at forty-nine, but he isn't that good anymore. He's just hanging on. And he'll be anxious. He knows who you are, he knows you've been well-coached and he's seen you shoot."

"What's his weakness?"

"Long shots."

"Well, that's true for most of us."

"You make 'em all the time."

"No, not all the time."

"Harley, you know the game. You see the table. You look at the balls left and you know which pockets they belong in. You do that better than I ever did."

"Then how come I don't always beat you?"

"Nobody *always* beats anyone."

Well, I knew that, of course. Losing, after all, is what you escape from.

"All you have to do is play your game. You've got one match before the lunch break. Play this one as if it were for the championship."

I nodded and Dad clapped me on the shoulder. "Go get him," he said and then walked back to his seat.

Well, I did. I was three games down when I got onto the table and then I hit my rhythm, sinking shot after shot, moving on to the next shot before the ball even dropped. My stroke was as deadly as a striking snake. Smokin' … absolutely, totally … smokin'.

I put my stick away and walked over to one of the lunch

tables reserved for players and suddenly there was this huge guy standing in front of me.

"You shoot some awesome pool, man."

"Hey, Joe, how you doin'?"

"Cool. Everything's cool. But, man, where'd you learn to shoot like that?"

"My dad taught me." I grinned. "Then I practiced."

"You got a shot at winning this?"

"Sure." I grinned. "How're the grades coming?"

He laughed. "You never let up, do you."

"Never do."

"I'm working hard. If I do okay in finals, I oughta have a B average." He looked surprised.

"And next semester you go for A's."

"We're gonna be in the state championships, you know. Hard to concentrate then."

"But that's what you're gonna face in college. Good to get used to it now. You need help, let me know."

"I can do that."

"How's the outside shot? You ready to try it?"

"I'm ready."

"Just set the pick, I'll go inside then turn and kick it back to you. You'll be wide open. Don't think. Shoot."

"Westport's got three big men. They play zone and a box and one. We're gonna be busy."

"Once you step out and sink a shot, they'll have to double

on you and someone is gonna be open. How fast are they?"

"Just big."

"Good. You gonna hang around?"

"Wouldn't miss it."

Mom and Janey showed up after lunch and Dad steered the conversation away from pool. I have no idea what we talked about. I might as well have been on another planet.

Then Soc turned up with April and Lottie. He was looking a little green around the gills, but he was there. Even Lt. Colello was there.

My stomach was running laps around my backbone. Sixteen players left, including four players ranked in the top ten in the country. I felt like I was trying to climb Mt. Everest without oxygen. Win three matches and I'd be in the final. Take the next four matches and I'd be champion. What a rush!

Nothing prepares you for playing at that level except playing at that level. My insides were churning, my head was spinning, and whatever focus I'd had before had faded to the point where I felt like a little kid who was first learning to walk, wandering from object to object and then hanging on. Not good.

I warmed up by making cross-side and cross-corner shots, working my way up the table and back until Shorty called for the next matches.

I got lucky and won the toss for the break which meant I went from practice to playing without having to wait. I ran the first rack to go one up and broke again but my stroke drifted slightly to the left and I only dropped one ball and left myself with a very difficult shot on the one ball.

The only out was a combination off the one into the seven and though I'd made harder shots, right then I knew I couldn't pull it off. Instead I played safe, kissing the one and burying the cue ball, leaving my opponent a four cushion shot or a safety.

But at that level, guys make four-cushion shots and that's exactly what Paul Scanlon did. He hit all four cushions perfectly with the cue ball before it hit the one, and sent it across the table to knock home the six.

I should have panicked. I should have collapsed. I should have, at least, begun to believe that I couldn't win. Not that it did me a whole lot of good just then because it wasn't my table and he'd gotten into a good solid rhythm, moving quickly from shot to shot and then ... unaccountably, he got ahead of himself. I saw it long before he shot.

So simple. He just didn't set his feet and then he tried to adjust and he was off balance when he shot.

Hello trophy, I said to myself as I chalked my cue and went to work. Game by game I shot myself into the lead and then into the final eight players.

I dropped onto a stool to wait for the next match to start and when I glanced up there was Roadkill. As I watched he bent over to pick something from the floor and I felt like someone had just dumped a bucket of ice water over me.

What I saw was the guy in the alley. I saw it in the way his shoulders rounded forward and the way he squatted down and then the way his shoulders pushed forward when he stood up. He was even wearing the same cap.

And then as he stood, Roadkill looked directly at me. His face showed no emotion, nothing. His eyes were cold and blank and dead and they were focused on me and no-where else. And then they changed and his face seemed to sag and he turned away quickly and walked out through the back door.

I slid off the stool and walked over to Soc, bent down and whispered in his ear.

"It's Roadkill," I said. And then something else clicked into place, the piece I had been missing from the start.

"How do you know?"

"He left when he caught me looking at him."

"He's not too tall?"

"I got that wrong. I forgot that the alley at Nicolo's slopes down from the street."

"So the guy would look shorter."

"Right." I shook my head. "I can't believe I did that."

"I'll tell Nick."

"Good." I looked around and now everything seemed sort of smoky, hazy as if the fog had moved in off the water and into the room.

I don't know how it is that you know when something is over, but I knew it then. I had to beat Tommy Sunday and it wasn't going to happen.

We shook hands before the match and, heck, it was a thrill even to shake hands with the top-seeded player in the country. But that didn't mean I was just gonna roll over.

The difference at that level is in the number of mistakes. I made the first one after going four games up and then … well, for me, it wasn't pretty. Tommy Sunday did what Tommy Sunday has done for years. He ran the table time after time and I never got to shoot again.

After the match he came over and shook hands. "Harley," he said, "the next time we play it'll be in a final match."

I smiled. "It was an honor, Mr. Sunday."

"The honor's mine, Harley. And I'll tell you something else. In my first big match I lost to your father."

"No way ..."

"You'll hear about it later when they interview me."

"Nobody here can beat you," I said.

"I know," he said. "You were the only one who could've."

And nobody did. He simply cleaned them up and I knew that if I had been a seeded player I wouldn't have played Tommy Sunday until the final match. It left me a lot to look forward to.

I did, however win the consolation match and I finished third and that was worth five thousand dollars. The guy who finished second got ten grand, and of course the winner took home twenty-five thousand.

After the presentations, I talked to Lt. Colello.

"What makes you so sure it's Roadkill?" he asked.

"He bent down to pick something up off the floor and he looked just like the guy in the alley, even the way he wears his hat."

He nodded. "But you never saw his face."

"No. And the time we picked up that guy in the storm. We never saw his face either."

"Roadkill's pretty easy to recognize," he said.

"But what if he dressed differently?"

"Could be. We'll keep an eye on him, anyway."

"He knows I know," I said. "I saw it when he looked at me and as soon as our eyes met, he left. I think he was the one in Black Springs too."

"Thanks for the help, Harley," he said, "and congratulations. Who knew we had a champion caliber pool player in town?"

I grinned back at him. "I did," I said. "And my dad."

He laughed. "Soc said you were cocky, but then maybe you've got something to be cocky about."

22 The Plan

Sunday night I loaded the software for Frenchy's system, rigged up the receiver and the antenna, and got it running. It seemed to work perfectly, except that the dot didn't move.

I zoomed in and it was on the right road in about the right place, but it was stationary. Which probably didn't mean much. I mean, how many people are out cruising around on a Sunday night when they have to get up early for work the next morning?

I switched to another screen and made some notes about what I knew, sticking to the facts, trying not to overlook anything.

Then I compared my list to the facts in the Black Springs story and discovered that I needed to know more. So I went on the Net and looked up the police department in Black Springs and e-mailed them about our situation, asking for any records they had about C. Renkler.

While I waited for a response I tackled my homework. Fortunately, there wasn't much to do and I got it out of the way and went back to Frenchy's software. The dot hadn't moved. He was at home ... or at least his mackinaw was at home. Maybe he was out somewhere, prowling around in that top coat. Why hadn't I thought of that before? I could have had Soc put a sensor on that coat too when he was in the house. Well, I could have if I'd had more than one sensor.

Or maybe the thing wasn't working. I walked to the window and checked the antenna. It looked fine, and I was certainly getting a dot on the screen.

For awhile I sat in the chair, my legs resting on the ottoman and stared at the screen and let my mind drift, the way I sometimes do when I'm tired. I let it fire at random, going from thought to thought until I drift back into real time.

And then I was thinking about the tournament. What surprised me most was not having fallen into a pit of depression over losing. A thing like that can weigh on you when you like winning as much as I do.

On the other hand, even in the past when the teams I had played for lost, I had never collapsed in grief. Instead, I went over what I could have done better, made notes, and worked on those things in practice.

And anyway, what was there to be sad about? I knew without a question, that I could play with the big boys. Two or three more tournaments and I'd solidify my ranking, get used to the level of play, and then maybe I'd be ready to win.

The next thing I needed to do was elevate my basketball skills until I could play with those big boys too, though to be honest, I didn't think that was possible because in basketball there are physical limitations. The question was whether I could make up for those limitations by the way I saw the floor and my skills as a passer.

But did I really want to play Division One? I knew the answer. I didn't. It was a game and I was not going to be an NBA player. Pool was different. Pool could go on. Basketball, for me, would end with college.

The dot moved. I blinked and then blinked again. It moved east down his street and then north on Centerville Road and finally turned west for several miles on Spring Hill Road and then stopped. I zoomed in. What the heck was up there? I had no idea, but I made a note and decided that tomorrow I'd darn well find out.

The dot stayed steady for perhaps fifteen minutes and then went back the way it had come and stopped at his house. Man, what a gadget!

At midnight I shut everything down and crawled into bed with one thing on my mind. I wanted to catch the killer. I even had a way to do it.

I picked up Soc in the morning and for about half the trip to school all I could talk about was Frenchy's system and how well it worked. The rest of the way we hashed over my plan and adjusted it to eliminate the obvious pitfalls.

Then we met at free period over coffee and worked it over again.

"Well." I said, "will it work?"

"I think it will. The question is when."

"We can't be there every night," I said.

"We don't need to. Right now we have a window. If he is a serial killer, he has to be ready and he was ready to nail us and he missed. That means he has to kill to take the pressure off."

"How's the arm?"

"Stiff and sore, but I can use it. He missed the tendons."

"Can you drive?"

"Yeah." He sipped some coffee. "Let's go over this again." He set the cup down. "You park your car at the Waterside Inn, with a manikin in the front seat dressed in a suit. Then we stake out the car with the camcorder and the tracking system and we wait."

"And that's the biggest hole. Once he knows he's been set up he'll run."

"But we'll have him on tape and that should make it easy enough for the cops to run him down."

"Depending on what kind of pictures we get."

"We can still track him with Frenchy's system. We'll be in a car in the parking lot and we'll track him and stay on him while we call the police."

"We need the pictures. Without them it could be anyone."

"Except that I can testify that I put the signaling device on Roadkill's coat," Soc said.

"It sounds good," I said. "It even feels good, but how will he know to look into my car, for example?"

"Only if he's looking for a victim."

"And we know he goes to the Waterside because that's where he had us drop him off."

We looked at each other and grinned.

"There are a lot of holes in this," I said.

"The problem is the timing."

"Well, we'll try tonight, anyway. See what happens."

"How about we take my shotgun along, tape him, and then blow him away. Or maybe just take his legs out." He grinned. "Or maybe we should get about fifty short guys all dressed in suits and ties to hide in the shadows and when he turns up we all jump out and his circuits will overload and turn him into a basket case."

I laughed.

"I just wish I could hold the shotgun," Soc said. "I owe him one."

It was a side to him I still didn't understand, and I wondered if that was the real reason why the bullies stayed away. Maybe they knew that he truly *was* dangerous and that he wouldn't stop once he got going. Could you know that about someone? It seemed to me you could but I had no evidence either way.

I'm a pretty aggressive guy when it comes to most everything, but as I told you, I'd given up fighting a long time ago and I was pretty sure I'd given it up because I wasn't any good at it.

"But no matter what," Soc said, "we don't try to stop him, physically, I mean."

I grinned. "And that's a good thing."

"No question about it."

That night I parked my car at the motel at about six. Soc sat in his mother's car, a pretty much ordinary Camry, about two rows away, waiting for me to finish.

I slid over to the passenger seat, pulled the mannequin out of the back seat, and put it in place behind the wheel. It wasn't a real mannequin like you see in a clothing store window. It was the dummy I'd made to decorate for Halloween at our last place and I made sure it went with us in the move.

The body was made of old panty hose stuffed with shredded paper and packed tightly. The head was the same, but I had drawn on ears and glued a wooden nose to the front and I'd gone to the barber shop and come back with a bag of hair which I glued in place.

But for this job, he got a suit straight from the Salvation Army store. He even got a dress shirt and a tie.

I turned on the dome light and arranged the dummy so

it looked like he was reading something. I'd even taken the precaution of putting on the Ohio license plates that I'd taken off the car when I registered it here.

Satisfied that everything looked okay, I walked back to the Camry and slid into the driver's seat. The camcorder was set up in the shrubbery on a tripod, aimed to get the best possible recording. I took the remote control from my pocket and set it on the dash. I'd already taped over all the little lights on the camera.

"How long should we wait?" I asked.

"No one was killed after nine o'clock," Soc said. "We'll wait till ten-thirty just to be safe." He opened the computer and I leaned over to look at the screen. It showed the map and the little white dot right where Roadkill lived.

For about fifteen minutes we sat there like idiots staring at that single dot and it never once even flickered.

"What if he wears a different coat?" I asked.

"Not likely. Every time I see him he's wearing that same old mackinaw. He even wears it inside. It's like he's afraid someone is gonna steal it."

At precisely quarter to nine, the dot began to move, slowly at first and then at a fairly steady clip as it followed along the roads marked on the map, headed right for us.

"Whoa, look at that," Soc said. "This thing really works."

I took out my cell phone and called Lt. Colello.

"Lieutenant, this is Harley Keene. Soc and I laid a trap

for the killer and it looks like he's gonna walk right into it. We've got a signal attached to his coat and we're tracing his movement on a computer. He should be here in no more than ten minutes." Then I told him what we had rigged and where we were.

"It'd be best if you could stay out of sight until I give you the signal. A block or so away would be okay, but not near the front of the Waterside. He'll be coming down Duck Hole, then turning onto Route One."

"Who are we talking about here, Harley?" he asked

"I'd rather not say until we're certain."

"Is this serious, Harley? I mean, you're not putting me on here, are you?"

"No sir."

"I need more information," he said.

"We think it's Renkler. I checked with the police in Black Springs and they say he lived there during the time when the murders occurred. He worked for the town crew."

"Why didn't they tell me that?"

"I asked them if they knew him?"

He sighed. "Look, just don't do anything foolish."

"Yes, sir. He just turned onto Route One."

"Okay, Sit tight. I'll be there as fast as I can."

I pointed to the computer. He was getting closer. When he reached a point two turns from the motel, Soc closed the computer so the light wouldn't give us away and I slipped out of the car and, keeping low, moved up to where I was sure the remote would work the camcorder.

The pickup stopped alongside the road in front of the motel and a big man in dark clothes climbed out, looked around, and then spotted the car with the dome light on and he circled and came up from the rear, smashed the window with his elbow, and drove a knife into the dummy.

The second the knife stuck home he knew it was a setup and he stood and looked around and I had him. I had a full frontal shot to go with the entire sequence.

And that's when somebody threw the chickens into the fan. A car coming from the other direction pulled into the motel and suddenly I was lit up like an actor on stage and he saw me. All I could do was run but not to the car, because Soc was there and he was in no condition to help and he was in the wrong seat to make a quick getaway.

I just hoped he wouldn't chase me. Yeah, right. No hope there. I ran — he chased. The thing about being chased in a situation like that is that the chaser is as dedicated to the pursuit as the chasee is to flight.

Fear, however, is a strong motivator and the more I ran the more my muscles warmed and slowly I began to gain distance. But it was clear that I'd have to run a long, long way before I dared try ducking to the side to let him go by.

I also didn't choose a very good route. I ran downhill toward the water. I don't know why. I just ran.

By the time we reached the piers I had gained but here there was absolutely no place to hide. There were the houses on one side and boats and the water on the other and out in front of me a quarter of a mile of absolutely straight road down to the dead end.

The only boat with lights on lay all the way at the end of the piers. The *Sea Wolf*. And then another nasty little thought popped into my head. What if the guy behind me wasn't Roadkill, but Black Jack Jones? No. The dot on the computer had started at Roadkill's.

That thought inspired me to run a little faster and when I looked back I'd gained again, but whoever it was behind me showed no sign of stopping or even slowing up. Somehow, I had to get away from him. I tried to think of something, anything, but by then fear was providing my energy and once that takes hold no rational or logical thought can compete.

Here's what I thought of. I called for help. I called out as loudly as I could and kept on running. It cost me some wind, but I continued to holler, getting closer and closer to the *Sea Wolf*, hoping that maybe Black Jack Jones would hear.

But when I reached his boat no one appeared and I was coming to the end of the piers and after that there was just water and to my right the solid rock retaining wall that rose up ten feet to the building above.

I reached back inside and found a few more miles per

hour and then I heard someone shout.

"Stop! Stop where you are! Stop or I'll shoot!"

When the gun went off I was sure I was dead. The second time it went off I began checking for holes. I stopped and looked back and I could see one man lying on the ground and another walking towards him with a rifle.

I pulled out my cell phone and dialed 911, wondering how I had managed to forget to do that while I was running. I guess I was just too busy getting away.

I walked back and in the streetlight there was Black Jack holding his rifle and looking down at the man on the ground, still alive and holding a great big knife.

"Let go the knife," Black Jack said. "Let it go or so help me I'll shoot you again."

In the light I could see the blood on the jacket, but the man's face was shielded by his hat. Slowly he let go of the knife and then he seemed to just settle onto the ground, lying flat against the cold pavement.

Black Jack walked around and kicked the knife well out of his reach, and then he looked around at me. "You okay?"

"I am now. I was about out of places to run."

"What the hell happened here?" Black Jack asked.

"That's Roadkill," I said.

"I know who he is. What I want to know is why he was chasing you with a knife."

"He's the killer."

In the distance we could hear the sirens.

"You're sure about that?"

"Absolutely."

"You saw him kill someone?"

I explained and he stood there looking at me and then shook his head. "You're even nastier when you aren't playing pool."

I shrugged.

"That was a compliment," Black Jack said.

And I guess, coming from him, it was. "Thanks."

He looked around and smiled. "It's good to have this done," he said.

I nodded.

"Sorry I shouted at you that day," he said. "Too grumpy for my own good sometimes. Comes from living alone, I guess."

I grinned. "You pretty much made up for that tonight."

"You ever go out fishing?"

I shook my head.

"Well, then, later, in the late spring when the blues come back, we'll go catch us a mess of 'em."

"I'd really like that."

So there it was. Another friend. Funny, the way things work sometimes.

A week or so later, Nick met with both our families at

Soc's house to explain what was going to happen.

Roadkill had been sent to a psychiatric hospital for evaluation and the word was that he'd never go to trial. He was, Nick said, a madman in every sense of the word. He had more crossed wires than a phone cable hooked up by a monkey. He'd spend the rest of his life in the hospital.

I got pretty worked up over that, I can tell you. I mean, all those people die and he gets to spend the rest of his life in comfort? Maybe as I grow older I'll understand the logic of that, but I don't think so. Some things just leave scars, and one of those scars belongs to Soc, a reminder of how close he'd come to being dead.

"Is there any chance he'll ever get out?" I asked.

Nick rubbed the back of his neck and then looked over at me. "In cases like this, there's always a chance. It's happened before. Some doctor puts him on medication and declares that as long as he takes the medication he can be released."

"You're kidding me," Mom said. "You can't be serious."

"Like I said. It's happened. But not this time."

"One thing I'd like to know," Soc said, "was whether he put the bullet through my truck."

"Maybe we'll find out later. Right now he's under such heavy medication that he can't be questioned."

"I don't understand," I said. "If he knew enough to try to get rid of witnesses, how crazy could he be?"

"The Attorney General's office is working on that," Nick said. "And the people in Colorado may try to extradite him. It seems that you gotta be crazier out there to escape a trial."

"Did you ever look at what's on Spring Hill Road," I asked.

Nick nodded. "He owned a piece of property there and there's a small barn on it. We found his father, or his father's skeleton inside. He'd been hanged."

Fifteen days later Roadkill Renkler died of an infection from the bullet wound. It seems that Black Jack's cartridges had at one time or another had been contaminated with the rotten fish he used to bait his lobster traps. I like to think of the dead fish as sort of like roadkills. Maybe I just like the irony. Mostly I just liked the fact that he was dead and things could get back to normal.

Funny. I had always thought of normal stuff as kind of boring. Not anymore.

In December we both heard from the colleges we'd applied to for early admission. Get this. That fox never told me he'd applied early to Bowdoin. So in eight months Soc and I would be going to Bowdoin and I thought that was about as cool as anything I'd ever heard. After all, we were both the weirdest friends each of us had ever found.